Miles Philson had his world nearly destroyed by a man who he should have been able to trust and look up to. Instead, it made him wary of forming connections of just about any kind. After joining the military, his brothers in arms helped him get past some of that, only to have that same general turn his life upside down all over again—by mutating him and his team into cheetah shifters and chemically altering their minds.

Once rescued from the general's clutches, Miles watches the other members of his team meet and fall in love with what the shifter world calls fated mates. When he meets wolf shifter Ron Reussmin and feels the pull, he understands what it means. The new feline presence in Miles's mind wants the boisterous, good-natured man, and Miles finally understands why his buddies didn't resist their new partners for long.

Unfortunately, Ron is a deputy in Stone Ridge, and they're going through some growing pains. An ex-employee is doing her best to stir up trouble. Can Miles keep his wolf shifter safe while staying off the radar of the shadow branch of the military that's searching for him and his team?

Having his Wolf's Back
Copyright © 2022 Charlie Richards
ISBN: 978-1-4874-3631-5
Cover art by Angela Waters

Published by eXtasy Books Inc

Look for us online at:
www.eXtasybooks.com

HAVING HIS WOLF'S BACK
WOLVES OF STONE RIDGE FIFTY-NINE

BY

CHARLIE RICHARDS

DEDICATION

When life gives you lemons, don't make lemonade. Make pink lem-
onade. Be unique.
~Wanda Sykes

CHAPTER ONE

M iles Philson stared at the small knot in the wood plank as he pounded out push-up after push-up. The colorful swirls of wood gave him a focal point, allowing him to shut down his mind and ignore the burn in his body's muscles. He breathed steadily, counting in his head.

Once Miles reached one hundred, he flipped to his back. He tucked his moccasin-clad toes under the bottom of his bed's footboard. Shifting down a little allowed him to bend his knees. Miles crossed his arms over his chest, found the gouges in the wood before him, and began an intense round of crunches.

Lifting and lowering, Miles ignored the rising burn in his abdominals. Instead, he wondered about the gouges. There were four of them, and they reminded him of something that could be made by claws. They were thick, like a canines.

"One-fifty," Miles muttered under his breath before flopping back to the floor. He panted roughly as he stared at the ceiling. "Holy shit."

Miles rubbed over his six-pack absently, trying to soothe the burning ache within his muscles. While he'd always worked hard to stay in shape while in the military, being turned into a shifter had cranked his fitness to a whole new level. His muscles recovered faster and stayed firm with less work, even though he pushed himself harder, too.

Ever since Miles was a teenager, he'd found working out to be a release. He could keep his mind focused on the activity as opposed to what was happening at home. The local gym

1

had been his safe place. It also helped with his goals—to become stronger, to be able to defend himself, to be able to stop the beatings, to—

The grumbling of his stomach yanked Miles's mind away from the direction his thoughts were spiraling—*thank god.* Along with enjoying increased physical fitness when being turned into a cheetah shifter, his appetite had increased . . . by a lot. When trapped by the scientists who'd created him, his free will stripped from him, he'd only been able to eat what and when he'd been ordered to. Miles has been hungry . . . a lot.

Now, though. I can eat what I want, when I want.

With that thought in mind, Miles rose to his feet. He grabbed his towel and his bath kit before opening his bedroom door. After a quick glance up and down the hall, finding it empty, Miles padded bare-chested to one of the two hall bathrooms.

Miles made quick work of his shower and morning routine. As much as many people exalted the wonders of coffee and how they couldn't start their day without it, he didn't agree. Instead, a quick workout to get his blood pumping woke Miles swifter and more fully than any cup of joe ever could. In fact, he skipped it most days, unless he was supposed to drink it to be polite.

And I normally don't worry about being polite.

With a slight smirk curving his lips, Miles pulled on a pair of faded blue jeans and a black shirt. He returned to his room and dropped his dirty clothes into his laundry basket. After pulling on a pair of socks and his combat boots, Miles headed back into the hall.

Inhaling deeply, Miles enjoyed the fragrant aromas filling the air as he headed toward the kitchen. His stomach rumbled appreciatively as he made out the scents of bacon, sausage, eggs, potatoes, and peppers. He wondered if the peppers had been included in the eggs or the potatoes. If Lark was cooking, they would be in the diced fried potatoes. If Nereo had taken over the kitchen, he would have added the veggies to the scrambled eggs. Both options were delicious.

Miles would miss Nereo's cooking soon. The vampire was mated with a fellow squad member — Warren. He'd originally been called in to help Miles, Warren, and the other two members of their squad — Crew and David — recover the memories that had been chemically stripped from them by the scientists who'd turned them into cheetah shifters. The vampire had immediately recognized Warren as his beloved — the vampire's term for what shifters called a mate, or fated soul mate. Due to Warren's desire to stay in the area with the other members of their squad, Nereo had chosen to resign his position as an enforcer to the Vampire Council, and they were in the process of house hunting. Nereo's identity was currently being reworked, and he planned to work as a deputy in the nearby town of Stone Ridge.

As Miles started down the stairs to the first floor of the lodge owned and occupied by Declan and Lark McIntire — the alpha wolf shifter and his human doctor mate — he was surprised to see neither man banging around the kitchen. Instead, he spotted Castrose Zukan moving around the space with confidence. Miles knew the human was also a fairly new arrival who'd originally been trained as a sniper in the Swedish military.

Miles had heard the story about how Castrose retired from the Swedish military only to peddle explosive devices created by his younger brother, Clayton. One of Clayton's devices had ended up in the hands of the human mate of the pack's head enforcer, who happened to be an ex-assassin. With a little magickal assistance from a warlock and his biker gang shifter friends, they'd located and caught Clayton.

Castrose had followed, searching for his brother.

Both men had ended up mated — Castrose to a wolf shifter,

and Clayton to Bailey Dyer. Bailey also happened to have been the commanding officer of Miles's squad. He'd been turned into a cheetah shifter, too, but Bailey's brother, Ronan, had secreted him away before the memory wipe had been completed. It was due to Bailey and the shifters that Miles and the rest of the team had been freed.

Thank god for that. Or the gods. Whatever you believe.

"Good morning, Castrose," Miles greeted as he reached the main floor. "I didn't realize you cooked."

"Not as well as Eion, but I can get the job done," Castrose replied, glancing over his shoulder at Miles before returning his attention to whatever was in the pan. "The coffee is ready if you want it."

"No thanks." Miles rounded the large dining room table that dominated the space between the stairs and the kitchen bar. When he spotted Castrose's arched brow—a silent question—Miles headed for the cupboard where he knew the tea was kept. "Not a real big fan."

"Hmmm." Castrose hummed and pointed toward a metal carafe keeping warm on a burner. "There's hot chocolate, if you'd prefer."

Holding a box of mint tea, Miles paused and considered that. "You know what?" He put the box back and closed the cupboard door. "I accept. I haven't had hot chocolate in years."

"You won't find better hot chocolate than Castrose's," Eion claimed as he strode into the kitchen. "Morning, Miles."

"Morning," Miles answered by rote as he grabbed a mug from another cupboard.

Seeing as Eion was busy giving Castrose a kiss, Miles didn't bother saying more just yet. Instead, he moved around them and grabbed the padded handle of the metal carafe. He poured the liquid into his cup, enjoying the aroma of the chocolaty brew.

After returning the carafe to the burner, Miles lifted the cup to his nose and inhaled deeply. "Mmmm." He hummed appreciatively. "That smells amazing."

Miles could hardly wait for it to cool enough to taste it. Still, he didn't want to burn his tongue, so he held off. Instead, he spotted a slight smile teasing the corners of the usually stoic Castrose's lips as he deftly flipped the hashbrowns in the pan. Eion, on the other hand, grinned broadly at him.

When Miles met the wolf shifter's gaze, Eion winked. "Told you. I almost don't bother with coffee anymore."

"Makes you taste better, too," Castrose teased, smirking at Eion. His attention lingered on his lover's lips for a few seconds before returning to his cooking.

Clearing his throat, Miles offered, "Can I help with anything?"

Eion moved toward the counter while holding up the bread. "Naw, we got it," he assured. "Just had to get the bread from my truck. Alpha Declan asked me to grab some on our way here, and I forgot to bring it in."

Miles nodded before heading toward the table. Resting in one of the chairs, he hazarded a sip of the hot chocolate. The warm, creamy chocolate goodness flowed across his tastebuds, making him smile with pleasure. Miles quickly swallowed the sip so he could enjoy a much larger mouthful.

Closing his eyes, Miles relaxed in his chair and just enjoyed the simple moment. He sipped his cocoa while listening to the sounds around him. With Miles having been turned into a shifter with heightened senses, everything seemed amplified . . . and maybe that was why he found his drink so amazing.

Miles heard the scrape of the plastic spatula on the pan. The bacon sizzled enticingly in another one. He even caught the slight creak of the floorboards under Castrose's boots. The sound of the toaster popping up seemed unusually loud.

"You okay there?" Eion asked, drawing Miles's attention.

Focusing on the wolf shifter, Miles watched him set a plate of toast as well as an empty one in front of him.

Miles nodded once. "Just processing the noise," he admitted. Seeing the questioning look in Eion's deep green eyes, he explained, "How much I can hear now is taking some getting used to."

Eion hummed as he nodded. "Ah." His smile appeared understanding as he scratched behind his ear, as if mentioning the noise caused his own ears to ring. "Yeah, it does take getting used to. It'll just take time. It makes enjoying the fresh mountain air even better." Wrinkling his nose, Eion added, "And remember to stay away from shifters with babies." He chuckled as he shook his head. "Visiting my siblings after they'd had their kids is a special kind of torture." With a snort, Eion admitted, "Suffice it to say, I'm glad my mate ended up a male, and they don't ask me to babysit."

Grimacing, Miles could only imagine. "Right."

"Feel free to get started on the toast. I'm making plenty more," Eion encouraged, waving a hand to indicate it. "Castrose is plating up the rest. Be right back."

Miles nodded and grabbed two pieces of toast. After placing one on his plate, he bit into the second, eating a third of it in one bite. Two more bites had him polishing off the buttered, crunchy goodness just as Castrose and Eion returned. Castrose placed a heaping mound of bacon and sausage links on the table along with a plate of golden-brown hashbrowns. Eion set a bowl on the table holding a mound of scrambled eggs with diced peppers in them. There was also cheese melting on top of the pile. While Castrose headed back into the kitchen, Eion placed a stack of plates on the table before he, too, returned to the kitchen.

As Miles took several strips of bacon and sausage links, he felt a little bad about serving himself while the guys who'd cooked the meal still plated the food. "You sure you don't need help?" he asked again even as he scooped a healthy portion of eggs onto his plate.

"I'm done here," Castrose assured, joining him with a handful of silverware and two mugs in his other hand. "Eion is starting more toast and buttering what just popped." He placed the bunch of silverware in the middle and assured. "Just eat. We're meeting Prier in half an hour," Castrose stated, surprising him. "You know what a stickler the asshole is for being on time."

"Meeting Prier?" That was news to Miles. "What for?"

Still, Miles began eating faster.

Castrose grinned broadly at him as he helped himself to a dollop of eggs. "Target practice."

Miles straightened, anticipation flooding him as his fingers twitched around the fork he'd just picked up. "Really?" He hadn't had the opportunity to handle a weapon since being moved to Stone Ridge almost a year before.

Smirking, Castrose replied, "Yep."

Miles ate eagerly.

Miles had enjoyed the hike through the woods in human form. After becoming a shifter, he'd mostly run as a cheetah. He'd nearly forgotten how invigorating a strenuous hike in the mountains could be.

The large feline he'd been granted grumbled a bit in the back of his mind, but he promised the beast he would run in cat form later.

So weird to be having a conversation with my other half.

Alpha Declan had assured him that he would get used to that, too.

Lying on his belly with Castrose's large sniper rifle in his grip, Miles peered through the scope. Castrose lay next to him, holding a pair of binoculars, acting as his spotter. Prier knelt on the other side with his own weapon resting on a tripod. The man had assured Castrose that he could shoot his rifle next.

"I'm seriously going to have to get one of these," Miles muttered as he prepared to squeeze the trigger. He anticipated the feel of the recoil of the rifle, and he had to take a few extra breaths to get his pulse under control.

"We'll do some online shopping," Prier assured, and Castrose could see the human's grin out of the corner of his eye.

"Hey, ten o'clock," Castrose stated, breaking the silence.

Miles panned to the left, searching for whatever had caught Castrose's attention. Prier's soft explicative told him that the human had found it first. When Miles spotted it, he growled softly.

A wolf hung upside down by his left rear leg, dangling in a pig snare.

"Do you know who that is?" Castrose asked darkly.

Prier grumbled under his breath for a few seconds before saying, "That's Ron Reussmin."

"The deputy?" Castrose sounded surprised. "How the hell did he get himself stuck in that predicament?"

"Hell if I know," Prier grumbled as he began straightening. "We better go help him."

"Wait," Miles murmured, spotting movement to the right. "There's someone coming up on him." Frowning as he took in the camo pants and black shirt, he eyed the knife sheathed at the slightly heavy-set man's hip and asked, "Do either of you know him?"

"Nope," Prier replied, a growl filling his voice, having returned his attention through his scope. "And look at that leer on the man's face."

"Wish we had comms and knew what he was saying," Miles grumbled, seeing the man's lips move.

"He said, so nice to see you, Ron. After I ransom your hairy ass to your pack, I'm going to sell you to the highest bidder."

Castrose finished his words on a growl. "Asshole."

"Okay then." Prier sounded way too calm. "Since he's obviously not there to help."

Miles understood perfectly. "I'll free Ron," he stated as he watched the wolf begin to growl and thrash, making the line holding him dance. "Just need the right second . . ."

Squeezing the trigger, Miles felt the jolt of the rifle before the sound of the gunshot even reached his ears. He appreciated the ear plugs the pair had given him in deference to his new heightened hearing. Just as Miles saw the wolf fall to the ground, the bullet having snapped the line, he heard Prier take a shot. In the next instant, the would-be ransomer collapsed to the ground.

While Miles couldn't hear it, his gaping mouth and the way he grabbed his leg told him that the guy was in considerable pain. The blood that quickly soaked his pants' leg confirmed it, too.

Prier patted Miles on the back. "Hell of a shot, Miles," he complimented. "Especially with Ron bouncing, making the string dance around." Then he rose to his feet. "Well, let's get down there before the asshole bleeds out," Prier stated, beginning to remove his rifle from the stand. "We'll bandage him up and take him to Alpha Declan."

"You bring a first aid kit?" Miles asked.

Prier nodded.

Miles began to strip as he stated, "Give it to me. I can get there fast. I'll be able to secure him, too."

"Okay."

Ignoring the way Prier smirked at him while staring blatantly as he finished peeling off his clothes, Miles crouched and shifted to his cheetah form. Then he took the strap Prier held out into his mouth before galloping into the trees.

CHAPTER TWO

R on Reussmin couldn't believe the indignity of what had just happened. Hanging upside down, staring at the ground five feet below him, he tried to figure out how the hell he'd missed the scent of the trap. Except, even dangling in the tree, Ron still didn't smell anything amiss.

Surely I should be able to scent the wire around my leg.

Except, Ron couldn't.

The snap of a twig drew Ron's attention to his left. He had to twist his neck awkwardly, but he managed it. Spotting a man in camo pants, a black shirt, and hiking boots, a slither of unease shot up his spine.

"So nice to see you, Ron," the man greeted, a cold grin curving his thick lips. His beady blue eyes were narrowed, and the glee in his expression chilled Ron to the bone. Ron began growling when the guy stated, "After I ransom your hairy ass to your pack, I'm going to sell you to the highest bidder."

Ron realized several things, and none of them were good. First, the guy knew about shifters. Second, he knew who Ron was, even in wolf form, and he knew his running routine. Finally, Ron was totally fucked, because he hadn't listened to his brother and hadn't told anyone that he was taking a run.

As the stranger approached, Ron caught a whiff of alcohol and something else . . . something . . . floral. Recognition teased at the corner of his mind, and he knew he'd smelled it before. Except, Ron just couldn't place it.

When the guy pulled a couple of cords from his pocket,

Ron growled loudly. He began to writhe in the air, ignoring the pain it sent streaking down his leg. Snapping his jaws, he made certain the asshole knew exactly what was going to happen if he got close.

To Ron's frustration, the dude laughed. "Yeah, Ron. Go ahead and struggle." He smirked as he used his hands to snap the cords a couple of times. "I'm going to tie your front paws together, then your jaws." Patting the knife he had strapped to his side, he continued, "Then I'll cut you down and watch you fall flat on your face before I finish hogtying ya."

Before the human could take another step, Ron heard what sounded like a gunshot in the distance . . . followed closely by a second one. He tensed, worried someone was shooting at him. Instead, Ron felt the cable holding him give way, and he tumbled unceremoniously to the ground.

"What the — " the guy who'd began taunting him started. His words cut off on his scream of agony as he sank to his butt. "Son of a bitch!"

Acting on instinct, Ron sprinted into the forest, limping on his left hind. It took him a few heartbeats, but he managed to curtail his need to flee. Ron paused, tipped his head to the side, and listened.

Ron could just make out the asshole still cursing a blue streak. Making out the sound of tearing cloth, he wondered what the man was doing. After that, Ron heard the sound of a stick breaking.

Knowing someone had gone through the trouble of shooting him down before trying to incapacitate whoever that was, Ron realized he had to make certain the human didn't manage to flee the scene. He began to trot back the way he'd come, but the pain flaring up his limb gave him pause. Peering at the cord still looped firmly around his hind leg, Ron sniffed at it before attempting to grip it with his teeth.

Growling with frustration when he couldn't get the neces-sary grip on it, Ron gave thought to the idea of shifting. Ex-cept, his human limb was quite a bit larger than his wolf one. He imagined the tight loop could do some serious ligament damage before he managed to get it off . . . assuming the pain didn't make him pass out first.

Ron growled softly as he began limping back the way he'd come. Doing his best to ignore the discomfort, he focused on the scents around him. When something earthy, masculine, and feline teased his senses, he wondered if a cougar was nearby, drawn by the smell of the asshole's blood.

Except, then Ron felt his arousal stir, along with a nearly irresistible desire to track down the owner of the pleasing aroma.

Shaking his head, Ron focused on returning to the area where he'd been snared. He figured he would have needed to fight his wolf harder, except, the smell seemed to be coming from that direction. Ron barely refrained from sprinting into the clearing once more, injury be damned.

Hearing the unmistakable sound of a deep growl, followed by the guy muttering, "Holy shit," Ron paused and peered through the trees.

Ron worried he would have to fight off said cougar in or-der to save the worthless human's ass. That would suck. To Ron's surprise, and relief, he didn't see a cougar creeping up on the guy. Instead, he saw a cheetah.

He knew there were five cheetahs in the area. They'd all originally been wholly human, a team of military elite, who'd been shown bogus videos about shifters intending to start a war to subjugate humanity. They'd been experimented on, and in the end, they'd been turned into cheetah shifters.

While Ron had met a few of the men while visiting his brother, Markus—who was mated to the older brother of one of the altered humans—he'd never seen any of them in their shifted forms. He had to say . . . the cheetah before him was magnificent. The cat was all lean lines and toned muscle.

Ron felt the sudden urge to trot out there, yip at the other shifter, and try to get him to play. That way, he would have an excuse to tackle him. He could rub up against him and enjoy more of that earthy, feline scent that was driving his senses crazy.

Oh shit! Is this cat my mate?

He nearly danced in place in his excitement at that thought. He'd been so damn jealous of Markus and all the others in the pack. Those around him had kept finding their fated mates, but he had not.

Now, I think it's my turn!

As Ron had been lost in thought, the cat had begun to shift. He was fairly quick, giving the human time to skitter backward a few feet and pull his knife from its sheath. Even in wolf form, Ron did a fair job of rolling his eyes.

Yeah. Like that's gonna help.

Ron watched as a gorgeous specimen of maleness rose from a crouch. He'd never met this man at his brother's place, and he greedily enjoyed the view.

The altered human's body was thick and powerfully built. He had muscles for miles, and his six-pack appeared to show the beginnings of an eighth. His blond hair was still cropped military short, and he had a scar bisecting his left brow, giving him an enticingly roguish appearance.

Ron wanted to lick and suck every inch of him. And considering the guy had to stand at least six-foot-four, there were plenty of inches to be had.

Yum!

"You can put the knife down so I can doctor your leg," the guy stated, yanking Ron out of his lustful thoughts. "Or I'll take the knife away from you, render you unconscious with the handle, and doctor your leg anyway."

"Why the hell would you help me?" the human asked, still

holding the knife between them. Sweat had formed on his brow, and his hand trembled. "You're one of *them*." He spat the last word as if it was some sort of curse.

"I'm not helping you," the altered answered calmly, picking up a small black bag with a red cross on the side. "I'm helping the guy you tried to kidnap." As he began slowly stalking forward, he glanced from the human's face to the knife and back again with a calculating gaze. "I'm going to take you to our pack alpha, and he'll decide the best way to get the truth of how you learned of shifters out of you."

"No," the man snarled, even as his features continued to pale.

"Yup," the altered growled. Then he lunged, using the first aid kit to batter at the man's hand that held the knife. The guy's grip must have been loose, weak, or just inexperienced, for the blade went skittering into the underbrush. "See?"

"You said you were going to use the handle to knock me out," the guy replied belligerently.

Unwilling to allow that asshole to call his mate a liar, Ron quickly retrieved the fallen blade. He eased from between the foliage, the knife handle in his jaws, and peered up at his altered human. With a soft, slightly muffled whoof, Ron drew his attention.

His mate turned his gaze upon him and grinned. "Hey, Ron. Thanks," he stated, revealing that he knew who Ron was, which pleased him to no end, and Ron barely resisted prancing with pride or wagging his tail like a damn dog. His mate began reaching toward him, his palm turned up to accept the knife. Freezing, his pale blond brows shot up, making the scar crease oddly. "Oh." He barely breathed the word as his nostrils flared. After licking his lips and swallowing so hard his Adam's apple bobbed, he murmured, "That's . . . unexpected."

Ron let out a mix between a growl and a whine.

The altered shifter completed the move, gently taking the handle from beneath Ron's teeth. "Not bad, Ron," he assured, with a slight smile. "Just unexpected."

"What's unex—"

His mate swung his arm and smacked the handle upside the human's head. "Shut up," he grumbled, shaking his head. He glanced Ron's way before kneeling, placing the bag on the ground before him. "You gonna shift, Ron? Seems we need to talk, hmm?"

Ron wanted to shift so damn badly, but he couldn't yet. Slinking forward, he sat on his furry butt. Then he eased his left hindleg forward, drawing attention to the snare loop still tight around him.

"Ah. Can't shift with that around your ankle, huh?" His mate seemed to understand immediately. He began reaching toward him before pausing and meeting his gaze. "This might hurt due to the circulation returning. Ready?"

Dipping his canine snout in a nod, Ron told his mate that he was ready.

"Okay."

Ever-so-carefully, his mate teased around the wire, obviously searching for purchase. He must have found what he wanted, for he managed to slip a blunt fingernail under the wire. Then he carefully held the slip-knot and fed the wire through, loosening the noose.

Just as his mate had predicted, pain surged through his limb as circulation returned.

Ron whimpered once before he could bite back the sound.

"Easy, Ron," the man murmured. "I know." Gently, he gripped his limb. "This should help. Just give me a minute."

Then, ever-so-gently, his mate began to massage his leg, helping to restore the blood flow.

Except, that wasn't the only thing it did to Ron's body. His blood flashed hot, and he barely managed to keep from

15

springing wood as a wolf. He shivered with pleasure, relishing the sensation of his mate caring for him.

Unable to wait a second longer, and no longer having a reason not to, Ron shifted. With the vestiges of pain still swimming through him coupled with the arousal, it took him a few extra seconds. By the time Ron finished, his mate had backed up a couple of feet. He rested his weight on one folded leg. He had his forward knee propped up, essentially hiding his groin.

Of course, that didn't stop Ron from scenting the wonderfully fragrant aroma of his mate's arousal.

Gods, he's delicious . . . and affected by me.

"So, we're mates," his mate commented slowly, clearly still a bit uncertain. "At least, that's what the cat in my mind is telling me."

"We're mates," Ron confirmed, eyeing the gorgeous man before him. "And you have me at a disadvantage." Offering his mate a wide smile, he stated, "I know you're one of Bailey's men, but what's your name?"

His mate smiled wryly at him. "Sorry about that." Holding out his hand, he claimed, "I'm Miles Philson."

To hell with a handshake.

Ignoring Miles's hand, Ron lunged forward. He clearly caught the military man off-guard, and they tumbled backward. With his mate sprawled under him, Ron felt every delicious inch of his strong altered human's frame.

"Hello, my mate," Ron crooned.

Dipping his head, Ron sealed his mouth over Miles's. He figured he must have surprised his mate, for the man gasped. Ron took complete advantage and slipped his tongue into the other man's mouth.

Ron groaned as he finally tasted heaven.

CHAPTER THREE

While Miles figured he should have expected it . . . he hadn't. The idea that the lithe handsome naked shifter would suddenly tackle him didn't even blip his radar. That being said, Miles hadn't thought of a guy—naked or otherwise—as handsome in a hell of a long time, either.

To be fair, Miles had always been able to look at a guy and judge him objectively. He needed to be able to evaluate others, and that was part of it. Handsome men used their looks to get their way just as often as beautiful women did. Accepting what was aesthetically pleasing and what wasn't was simply part of his training.

That being said, Miles had never kissed a guy.

Until now, anyway.

Ron had his lips on Miles's so fast, his head nearly spun. Either that or it was the pheromones his cat side was obviously picking up on. The damn beast was purring contentedly, happy to know their wolf wanted them so badly.

Miles opened his mouth as he gripped Ron's shoulders, intending to push the man back and express his reservations. Except, in the next instant, he found his mouth full of Ron's tongue. Miles tightened his grip, once again intending to ease the man away.

Except . . . then Ron's flavor finally registered on his taste buds.

Fucking hell.

Delicious.

Miles had never tasted anyone so . . . amazing. Ron's flavor was a mixture of the hot chocolate he'd drank that morning and something masculine and wild . . . like a really wild berry wine. While Miles had no idea how it was possible, it totally worked, and Ron tasted beyond amazing.

Holy shit! How is this possible?

Unable to help himself—and with his cat's purring urging him on—Miles teased his tongue along Ron's appendage. He slowly engaged in the tongue-play, licking and nipping. Miles slid one hand up and threaded his fingers into Ron's thick, light-brown hair. Gripping gently, he used the hold to ease Ron's head back a little, allowing him to end the kiss.

Peering into Ron's hazel eyes, Miles saw how the brown had darkened to dominate his irises, betraying his desire just as much as the pheromones pouring from him. The wolf shifter was also panting harshly, and his nostrils were flaring, telling Miles that the shifter was enjoying his scent. Miles would have been embarrassed about the fact that he was aroused as hell from their lip-lock—his cock hard as nails and twitching against his abdominals—but he could feel Ron's answering hard-on pressing against his hip.

Plus, while Miles had been wondering how shifters tolerated their heightened senses only that morning, the way the heady scents of their arousals combined in his nostrils set his blood damn near on fire.

"Holy shit," Miles mumbled, ever-so-eloquently. Seeing Ron's wide smile and kiss-swollen lips, he had the sudden urge to dive right back in again. He barely resisted as he muttered, "Wow."

Ron grinned broadly, obviously pleased that he'd managed to render Miles to one-word mutterings.

"I—"

"Well, isn't this interesting," Prier's tenor voice drawled. "Did you plan to let the asshole bleed out while you and Ron fucked? Not that *I* would mind too much. Plus, the view would be lovely." The head enforcer's mate scoffed before adding, "Sadly, questioning him is sort of important."

"You're a dick," Castrose commented in an almost conversational tone.

"Yes, I know," Prier replied without missing a beat. "So, where did you drop the first aid kit? Ah, there it is." He patted Miles's bare upper thigh. "Mind lifting a bit. I need to grab this."

Miles could feel Prier grabbing more of his thigh before he focused on the bag, and he growled with annoyance.

Sadly, all that did was make Prier laugh.

Ron seemed to take exception. He glared at the enforcer's mate and snapped, "Damn it, Jared. Stop feeling up my mate."

Prier lifted his free hand even as he snickered.

"Who's Jared?" Castrose asked, stating what Miles was also wondering.

Huffing a sigh, Ron pointed at the hazel-eyed human mated to the head enforcer, who they knew as Prier.

The human smirked and shrugged. "Many are still getting used to the name Prier." He winced, adding dryly, "Including me." With a sigh, he began sorting through the med-kit as he knelt next to the unconscious asshole. "I had my ID adjusted to read Prier Jared Bozeman. That way, if someone slips up, I can claim it's my middle name, and my driver's license will be proof of that."

Castrose sighed deeply, sounding annoyed. "Jared. Jared Templeton."

Spreading his arms wide, Prier bowed at the waist while still on his knees. "With pride."

Nodding as if all his questions were answered, Castrose muttered, "Now everything that's happened makes sense. You and the paranormal." He scowled as he shook his head. "You were supposed to die for your crimes as a casualty of one of Clayton's bombs."

Lifting his arms and shoulders in a *what can you do* shrug, Prier grinned. "Surprise. I can't imagine why Clayton didn't tell you that his information about me had been contrived. Damn rogue wolf shifter and still on the run."

Prier's anger bled through as he muttered the words while rummaging through the first aid kit, making Miles realize the human mate still dwelled on something Miles wasn't privy to. Before he could even begin to think of where to start with questions—after all, his head was still swimming with arousal—Prier turned his attention to the asshole unconscious on the ground.

"Well, I'll stabilize his leg first, then we're going to need to carry him back." Prier smirked as he glanced between Miles and Ron. "I'd originally intended for one of you shifters to carry him, seeing as you're stronger than us, but"—he waggled his eyebrows—"the view sure is nice." Even as Ron growled, Prier continued, "Do you want lube, Miles? I figure you've had a hell of a dry spell, seeing as you couldn't even take a shit without permission after those scientists fucked with your head." As Prier talked, he inspected the unconscious asshole's leg and began pulling things from the first aid kit. "I can rig up a litter real quick, and Castrose and I can leave you to your fun with Ron."

Then Prier blinked once, and he snapped his attention to Ron, a roll of bandages in hand. "Wait a sec." He narrowed his hazel eyes as he glanced between them. "Did you say mate?" Cocking his head, Prier continued, "Miles is your mate, Ron?"

"Yeah," Ron responded, a growl in his voice. "Miles and I are mates."

Arching one brow, Prier pinned a questioning look on Miles. "Miles? Do you recognize Ron as your mate?"

Miles swallowed hard even as his mouth went dry. After a glance at Ron, taking in his expectant expression, he knew there was no way he could deny the wolf shifter. Returning his attention to Prier, Miles dipped his head in a curt nod.

Still, Miles knew that he couldn't leave it there. "Yes, Prier," he confirmed, claiming a man—shifter—as someone he intended to . . . be with. After all, it was the shifter way. As Miles's cat rumbled with pleasure at his admission, he added, "And no, we don't need any lube." Upon seeing Ron's furrowed brows, he added, "And I'll carry him back. You have my clothes?"

I could use the time to wrap my head around this development.

To Miles's surprise, Ron growled softly. "You just claimed me, and now you're walking away?"

"No," Miles quickly denied. Confused, he asked brusquely, "Where the hell are you getting that?"

"You're using busy work to put space between you and Ron right after you've met him," Castrose pointed out, shaking his head. "Stay with him. You've been a shifter for months. If you have reservations or problems, talk it out with him." Turning his attention to Prier, Castrose stated, "I'll just carry the asshole over my shoulder."

Prier glanced over his shoulder at Castrose and, smirking, nodded once. "Sure, man. I'd be happy to watch your muscles strain as we hike back."

Rolling his eyes, Castrose crossed his arms over his chest. "As you know, there's a service road a mile and a half to the west. It's probably where this asshole hiked in at." He jerked his chin in the direction of the unconscious man. "I've already texted Eion. He's meeting us there with a pack truck."

To Miles's confusion, Prier snickered. "And I was getting a kick out of being a cock-blocker for a change." Then he winked at Miles and rose to his feet. At the same time, he tossed something on the ground near Miles's face. "Let's go, Castrose."

As Prier packed the first aid kit, Castrose strode over and easily lifted the human into his arms. A moment later, the pair started away from them.

That was when Miles realized what Prier had left on the ground for him—a single-use packet of lube.

Before disappearing between the trees, Prier turned and leered at him, winking lewdly. Then they were both gone.

A second later, Ron snatched out a hand and grabbed the lube.

It suddenly hit Miles. The entire time Prier and Castrose had been there, he'd lain underneath the wolf shifter. He frowned, focusing on Ron, who was eyeing the packet of slick with interest. When Ron grinned at Miles and wiggled the object, Miles growled and shook his head.

"I said we didn't need that out here," Miles snapped.

Ron's expression turned crestfallen. "You don't want me?" he whispered as he furrowed his brows. He even shook his head once, as if trying to shake free his disbelief. "But you admitted we're mates. I . . . I don't understand."

Realizing how his brusque words could have sounded, Miles quickly assured, "I'm not rejecting you." When Ron blinked at him with his deep hazel eyes, his expression questioning and hopeful all at once, Miles continued, "I just—" He hesitated a heartbeat, then told the wolf shifter, "We're mates, and I don't intend to bond us in some hurried frenzy on the forest floor." Miles ignored the grumblings of his cheetah as he continued, "I want a bed. I deserve a bed." Frowning, he met Ron's expressive eyes. "And, damn it, you deserve a bed, too."

"I, uh . . . okay." Ron sounded confused as hell.

Damn. What the hell kind of lovers has Ron been with in the past?

Miles wasn't certain he wanted to know the answer to that question.

"So." Miles bucked his hips a little even as he rubbed his palms down Ron's sides. "Um, how about you get up, and you can lead me to your place?"

That seems reasonable enough, right?

To Miles's relief, Ron grinned widely, clearly pleased. He pressed a hard kiss to Miles's lips before easing away from him. Then he began to shift, the tell-tale pop and crack echoing off the trees as he changed shape.

Realizing Ron expected to run home in animal form, Miles decided to roll with it. He began his own transformation. Besides, he figured the run would give him a little time to figure out how to admit his ignorance to his clearly experienced mate.

Once back in cheetah form, Miles watched as Ron bounced around him for a moment. Miles could just stand there in awe as he took in the wolf's seemingly boundless energy. The wolf finally paused and sidled close to him, a question clear on his canine features. Ron's wolf ducked its head, his tail wagging slowly, and there appeared to be uncertainty on his canine features.

For a few seconds, confusion filled Miles. Then . . . it hit him. Wolves were very social creatures. They liked to play—tumbling and romping with each other. Not to mention, mates were supposed to be affectionate in animal form, too.

Or so I've heard.

Doing his best to relax, Miles eased forward and lowered his head. He sniffed at Ron's jaw, then his ear. To his surprise, he found the masculine scent mixed with wolf to be pleasing. When Miles felt his cat's need to rub his scent against the wolf, Miles went with it. Tipping his head, he rubbed along the beast's jaw, then down his neck, and over his shoulder.

Miles found it felt nice, good, pleasant even. Especially when Ron rumbled soft and returned the nuzzling. Miles had never felt anything so . . . nice . . . relaxing . . . and if he'd been in human form, he wasn't certain he would have found words to describe it.

Fortunately, as a cat, Miles didn't have to try.

After a couple of moments of what Miles acknowledged

was them rubbing their scents on each other, Ron finally drew back. The wolf yipped once, then turned and began jogging into the forest. He paused once, his tail wagging, his expression entreating him to follow.

Miles did so.

After a twenty-minute jog through the forest, Miles followed Ron through a break in the trees. He saw a small cottage situated in a clearing. The grass had been recently mown, and the structure appeared to be in good repair, telling Miles that Ron took pride in his home.

Ron slipped through a doggie door off the back porch, and Miles paused. Staring at the square door, he wasn't certain he could fit through there. Fortunately, a human-shaped Ron opened the door and peered at him.

Grinning, naked and obviously comfortable with it, Ron stepped back and swung the door wide. "Wanna shift and enter?"

After a second of hesitation, knowing what Ron expected to come next, Miles shifted. Back in human form, he rose to his full height, discovering he had a good four inches and fifty pounds on the wolf shifter. That didn't help with his uncertainty as he moved slowly into Ron's house.

Hearing the door close behind him, Miles turned. He saw the heated gleam in Ron's hazel eyes as he strode toward him, and a mixture of hunger and unease slithered through him. When Ron moved close, Miles gripped his shoulders. He held him steady, not letting him get *too* close.

"Miles?" Ron asked questioningly. He lifted his hands as if to touch him, but he hesitated. "Uh . . . talk to me?"

Evidently, Ron finally caught on to Miles's uncertainty.

Bowing his head for a second, Miles tried to sort his own thoughts. "So much has happened in just a few minutes," he mused softly, furrowing his brows. Lifting his face, he focused on Ron. "I wasn't born a shifter, and I'm trying to catch up with these . . . desires."

Ron cocked his head, clearly trying to understand. His brows creased as he murmured, "Are you . . . not, uh" — he licked his lips, drawing Miles's attention to them and reminding him of how good the man tasted — "not gay, uh, or bisexual?"

Miles forced himself to focus on the question rather than the desire that simmered through him . . . especially since he didn't actually know what to do about it.

And that's what I need to explain.

"I've always considered myself bisexual," Miles admitted for the first time in his life. Fighting back the heat that threatened to warm his cheeks, he forced himself to hold Ron's gaze as he added, "But I've never done anything with a guy." As Ron's features began to relax, Miles felt his own tension ratchet up again. Unable to help himself, he blurted, "I want you, but I'm going to need a little time."

Watching the expressions dance across Ron's features, Miles wished he could read scents, but it wasn't something he'd taken the time to figure out yet.

To Miles's relief, Ron smiled warmly and told him, "As long as you're not rejecting me, time is something I'll be happy to give."

Miles offered Ron a small smile of his own. "I'm not rejecting you." Rubbing over his closely-shorn scalp, he admitted, "I, uh . . . I want this, too." While Miles had never had a relationship, he'd watched all his buddies find bonds, and they seemed happy about it. He wanted that for himself. "I'm sure it won't take me long to figure my shit out."

At least, I hope not.

Ron beamed at him, his dark eyes glittering. Taking Miles's hand, he tugged at him gently. "Then let's get comfortable, and we'll learn more about each other."

While Miles wasn't certain what that meant, he still nodded and followed the wolf shifter deeper into his home.

CHAPTER FOUR

R on couldn't believe his good fortune. Not only had Fate given him a sexy-as-fuck mate, the man was open to being with him. While his wolf grumbled in his mind at the thought of waiting, Ron mentally shushed his animal.

Our mate needs time. We can give him that. At least we don't have to explain paranormals, mates, or bonding with him. Miles already knows.

With his wolf settled, Ron led the way down the hall, past his spare bedroom—which he'd set up as an office—and the hall bathroom. He appreciated that Miles didn't hesitate to follow him into his bedroom and liked that his mate didn't seem to mind him holding his hand even more. With part of his attention focused over his shoulder at Miles, Ron caught the tick in his jaw as he glanced from the bed, swept his gaze around the room, then returned his attention to the bed.

Yup, there's definitely tension in his shoulders now, too.

Realizing his mate wouldn't be comfortable lying with him just yet, Ron decided on another course of action. "After a run, where I get sweaty and dirty, I like to enjoy a long, hot shower."

Ron pivoted and began walking backward in the direction of his ensuite. Unable to help himself, he found his attention drifting to Miles's prick. The sight of his mate's thick, probably ten-inch dick caused his chute to clench and his mouth to water.

Patience.

Forcing his attention back to Miles's fair features, Ron

hoped his smile appeared encouraging and not lecherous. "Will you join me?" Squeezing Miles's hand lightly, he added, "I would very much like the chance to wash your back."

To Ron's surprise — and pleasure — Miles's lips curved into a small smirk. "Just my back?" he quipped.

"I'll wash anywhere you let me," Ron murmured, unable to help the way his voice lowered to a husky rumble. He glanced toward Miles's cock again. When Ron spotted it twitch, his own engorged organ gave an answering jerk. Meeting Miles's crystal blue eyes once more, Ron added, "It'd be my pleasure."

Miles licked his lips, wetting the full plump flesh that Ron had enjoyed ravishing not too long ago. Recalling the way his mate had frozen for several seconds, he realized it now made sense. Pride filled him to know that he'd given his mate his first guy kiss.

We'll be doing a lot of firsts together.

Hell, yeah.

Anticipation thrummed through Ron, causing his dick to ache even more.

Patience.

"Actually, I'm feeling this unexpected need to take care of you," Miles admitted, lifting his free hand to rub at the back of his neck. He glanced down, past Ron's prick, and focused on his leg. "Are you okay? You seem to be moving just fine."

Ron smiled, a new kind of pleasure filling him. "Yeah," he assured, squeezing Miles's hand again. Ron glanced at his leg, seeing a faint red line just over his ankle, heralding where the trap had snared his leg. Resting the tips of his fingers on his free hand on Miles's jaw, Ron exerted a smidge of pressure so his mate once again met his gaze. "I'm fine. Once the cable was off my leg, I healed almost immediately. The line will be gone in less than an hour, I imagine."

Miles blew out a breath, then nodded. "Okay." He glanced over Ron's shoulder before refocusing on him. "I already had a shower this morning, but taking one with you . . . that would be nice." His cheeks took on just the faintest of pink. "Showered with the guys in my unit, but I bet this'll be different."

Ron smiled widely. "*Very* different," he vowed.

After swallowing hard, causing his Adam's apple to bob, Miles nodded again.

"Come on," Ron urged, moving again now that he'd procured his mate's acquiescence. "I had a new hot water heater installed two years ago." Leading into the bathroom, he indicated the jetted tub. "When I remodeled the bathroom."

"Oh, nice," Miles muttered, eyeing the large vessel.

"I'd love to share it with you sometime," Ron offered even as he opened the shower door. "But for now" — he reached in and started the shower — "let's enjoy this instead."

Once the temperature was right, Ron slipped into the large, tile stall. He eased halfway under the spray, then turned and beckoned to Miles. Ron watched as Miles flexed and released his jaw muscles for a heartbeat before he stepped into the stall with him and closed the door.

"Hello, my mate," Ron murmured as he took his loofah off the rack he'd hung on the wall. "Thank you for joining me."

Miles tipped his chin in the faintest of nods. Half under the spray, he stood, tension thrumming through him.

After pouring body wash onto the loofah, Ron began massaging up a lather. "May I touch you, Miles?" While he'd jumped the man in the forest, he realized that, at this point, getting his mate's permission would be a good thing.

Nodding once more, Miles murmured, "Yeah." He hesitated for a second, then added, "As long as I can touch you, too."

"I'd like that very much," Ron replied softly, enjoying the heat as well as the intimate moment.

Miles glanced around the space and grabbed the wash

cloth. He poured a dollop of body wash onto the already soaked fabric. Once he'd worked up a lather, he mirrored Ron. Together, they rested their respective scrubbers on each other's pectorals and began a slow rubbing.

The first touch of the cloth over Ron's skin caused his nipples to bead. As Miles slid the soapy fabric over him, his skin goose bumped, regardless of the heat, and his stomach clenched as butterflies bumped within. Ron reveled in his mate's gentle ministrations, hesitant though they were.

Ron rested his free hand on Miles's skin where he'd already soaped and began working the suds over his mate's skin. The feel of the firm flesh beneath his palms caused the hairs on his arms to stand on end. He focused on breathing slowly and deeply as he washed Miles, struggling to keep his raging arousal in check as Miles worked his way down Ron's chest.

When Miles reached his groin, he hesitated before wrapping the cloth around Ron's erection.

The move ripped a grunt of enjoyment from Ron, and Miles glanced at his face. "This okay?" he asked huskily.

"More than," Ron ground out, barely resisting the urge to pump his hips. Still, he couldn't help but plead, "Please do something."

His words spurred Miles on, perhaps bolstering his confidence, and his mate began using the cloth to jack his erection. The soft fabric sliding over the sensitive skin of his aching erection sent sparks up his spine. His cock flexed and jerked in Miles's grip, and his balls began to tighten.

Needing something to ground him, Ron dropped the loofah. He gripped Miles's upper arms. Clinging to the larger man, Ron began rocking his hips, chasing the friction and sweet sensations cascading through his body.

Miles focused on Ron's face once more, and a feral smile creased his lips. He eased a step closer, putting their bodies nearly flush and causing Ron's sensitive cock head to tap against Miles's ripped abdominals with every stroke. Then Miles cupped Ron's jaw with his free hand and rested his forehead against his own.

Peering into Miles's blue eyes, Ron saw the hunger within them. He could imagine he saw the man's cheetah staring back at him. His heart nearly pounded out of his chest as the intimacy of the moment caused his blood to burn in his veins.

"Come for me, my mate," Miles rumbled.

Ron was helpless but to obey. He moaned as sweet heat erupted throughout his body. His balls pulled tight, and his cock pulsed, expelling his seed in harsh, bliss-inducing spurts. Black spots danced across his eyes at the intensity of his release, and for a few seconds, his vision blurred.

"Gorgeous," Miles murmured before chuckling huskily. "Never thought I'd say that about a guy coming all over me."

Blinking a few times, Ron refocused on Miles. He spotted the smug smile on the blond's face and couldn't help but return it with a grin of his own. Ron hummed as he massaged Miles's impressive biceps, hoping to soothe if he'd gripped too tightly.

"I'd apologize, but it's your fault," Ron teased, grinning up at Miles. When Miles smirked, he noticed the hunger still in his mate's eyes. A glance down reminded him that his cheetah was still in need. "Your turn."

Ron didn't wait for permission. Easing to his knees, he gripped the base of Miles's erection. He peered up at Miles as he opened his mouth and leaned forward.

The wide-eyed expression on Miles's face, the way his nostrils flared in anticipation, spurred Ron on. He wrapped his lips around his mate's cock head, gratified to hear his sharp intake of breath. Tipping his head to just the right angle, Ron leaned forward and swallowed Miles's shaft to the root.

Miles's bark of surprise, followed by a low growling moan

as Ron sucked his way partway off, was music to Ron's ears. He began a slow, sucking bob, licking and teasing over Miles's silky hard flesh with his tongue. Gently, Ron cradled his mate's ball sack, testing his sensitivity.

"Ron." Miles practically hissed his name as a shudder went through his body. "Oh, fuck."

That was all the warning Ron received. In the next instant, his mouth was flooded with warm, salty cream. He quickly swallowed the thick burst as he half pulled off, readying himself for the next volley.

As Miles spurted burst after burst of the best-tasting cum Ron had ever had the pleasure of enjoying, he hummed his appreciation. He lapped over his forever love's crown while skimming his fingertips over his ball sack. Ron even teased his fingernails through his thin pubic bush, doing everything he could to extend his mate's pleasure.

Finally, Miles gripped Ron's neck and jaw, gently pushing him back.

Tipping his head up, Ron smiled with satisfaction upon seeing Miles's heavy-lidded, sated expression. The relaxed smile curving his mate's full lips was a sight that he wanted to put there often. He realized, at some point, Miles had ended up leaning his back against the wall for support, and Ron reveled in the knowledge that he'd made his mate weak-kneed.

"Come up here, Ron," Miles encouraged, sliding his hands to his shoulders and squeezing. "Time for another kiss."

More than on board with that, Ron rose to his feet. He rested his palms on Miles's hips as he leaned close. Ron tipped his head up in invitation.

Miles smiled at him for several seconds, his blue eyes glittering with something Ron couldn't read. Then the bigger man slid his arms around his waist. Tightening his hold, he pulled Ron flush against him. Miles lowered his head and sealed his lips over Ron's.

31

There was no hesitation in Miles that time.

Instead, Miles took the lead. He thrust his tongue into Ron's mouth, ravishing him with languorous strokes. Miles mapped him as if needing to learn every inch of him.

Ron enjoyed every second of it. Teasing his tongue against Miles's, he reveled in his mate's exquisite flavor. His body heated anew, gearing up for round two. His prick, which had barely softened to half-mast, thickened swiftly.

With a groan, Miles broke the kiss. He rested the back of his head against the shower wall as he panted heavily. With kiss-swollen lips, he smiled wryly at Ron.

"Kissing you is—" Miles paused and scoffed. "No words." Then he rocked his hips, pressing his hard cock against Ron's stomach. "But it sure feels good."

Groaning, Ron answered the move by rutting over Miles's thigh. "Definitely amazing."

"Mmmmm." Miles hummed, spreading his legs a little. The move lowered his height, aligning their bodies perfectly. "There," he muttered before tucking his nose against the side of Ron's neck. "Smell so damn good."

Ron moaned, tipping his head to the side, essentially submitting to the larger man. When he'd thought about finding his mate, he'd always assumed he would be the more dominant. Submitting to Miles, however, felt as natural as breathing.

Sliding his arms under Miles's arms, Ron gripped the backs of his shoulders. He clung, losing himself in the rising heat between them. The base of his spine tingled, and he knew it wouldn't be long before he unloaded a second time.

"Miles," Ron moaned his mate's name as he tipped over the edge. Ecstasy flooded him, and he shook in Miles's hold as he came all over again.

"Mine," Miles growled against his neck.

Ron smiled, feeling a little loopy. Still, he managed to mutter, "Yours."

An instant later, Ron felt teeth pierce his neck. A sharp stab of pain caused him to gasp. A second later, tingles erupted on his flesh. His beaded nipples tightened further, and his gut clenched.

A third orgasm crashed over Ron, sending his senses reeling. The spots that had threatened earlier returned in full force. As ecstasy weaved through Ron, his vision dimmed. In the next second, he felt himself float away on the waves of bliss, and he knew no more.

Ron roused slowly, warm and comfortable and his mind a muddle. He pried open his eyelids and blinked a few times to focus. He found himself curled up in bed on his side. Pale, thickly muscled arms were wrapped tightly around him, and a big body was spooned up behind him.

My mate.

"Welcome back, Ron," Miles rumbled into his ear before beginning to mouth kisses down his neck.

Smiling, Ron turned his head just a little, not wanting to dislodge Miles's magick mouth.

"Thanks." Ron chuckled huskily. "Never passed out from—" Recalling what had prompted it, he gasped and jerked a little. Ron twisted on the bed, although Miles didn't let him go far, tightening his arms to keep him close. "You started our bond."

Miles returned his regard steadily. "Yeah." He didn't sound or scent of any sort of regret. "That's what mates do, right?"

"Yeah," Ron replied softly, his shock beginning to ease upon seeing Miles's relaxed acceptance. Scoffing softly, he admitted, "Just didn't think you'd want to right away."

After shrugging one big shoulder, Miles urged Ron to roll fully. A moment later, he found himself tucked up against the man, half sprawled on top of him. His head rested on Miles's shoulder, allowing him to peer into Miles's clear blue eyes.

"Was I not supposed to do that, yet?" Miles asked, his pale blond brows drawing together.

"I'm over the moon that you started our bond," Ron admitted, grinning at him. "I just . . . you said you needed time."

Miles nodded. "Time to accept fucking a guy. Not time to accept our mate-bond." He offered him that small half-smile again. "Sounds stupid maybe, but I watched all the other guys in my unit go through it. Some fought it. Some accepted it right away." Lifting a broad hand, Miles teased his fingers through Ron's wet hair. "Better to accept and get to the good stuff." Appearing confident, Miles stated, "I'll talk to Warren or Bailey about ass fucking. Get my head around it. Then I'll claim you properly."

Ron gaped for a few seconds upon hearing Miles's confidently spoken words and scenting his certainty. A second later, he couldn't help but ask, "Can't you talk to me about, uh, fucking?"

Inhaling deeply, Miles squinted at him for a second before letting it out again. "Don't take this the wrong way, Ron," he began slowly, obviously choosing his words carefully. "I got a trust problem. We'll get there, uh, me trusting you, but I'm not there quite yet, and I need to talk this out with someone I trust." Even as a stab of hurt hit Ron full in the chest, Miles tightened his hold on him and muttered, "Damn, I'm fuckin' this up already. I don't mean to hurt you."

Ron rubbed a palm over Miles's chest, allowing the contact to soothe them both. "You're not fucking anything up," he assured, meeting Miles's gaze. Mentally, he released the pain caused by his mate needing to speak to another about sex. Instead, Ron stated, "You're right. We don't know each other." He smiled. "We'll get there."

Miles nodded once, looking relieved. "Yeah. Thanks." Relaxing on the pillow, he offered, "So, let's talk a little. Tell me about yourself, Ron. How old are you? How many lives have you lived so far?" Miles smirked as he added, "When should I move in?"

Barking a laugh, Ron grinned at Miles's brazenness, which he totally liked. "You can move in immediately." Then he shared that he was one-hundred-thirty-five years old, and he was working on his third identity.

They'd been chatting for nearly an hour when the alarm on Ron's phone buzzed, making it vibrate where he'd left it on the nightstand before his run.

Groaning, Ron realized his time with Miles was up for a while. "I gotta go to work," he explained as he eased away from his altered human.

Miles immediately released him and swung his legs over the side of the bed. "I understand work." He stood and peered out the window. "I'll run home and start packing. Which way is the alpha's house?" Returning his attention to Ron, Miles asked, "What time do you get off?"

Grinning, Ron told him, "I'll loan you a pair of sweats and drop you off at the alpha's." He crossed to the dresser to do just that. "And I get off at ten tonight. I'll give you a house key so you can get in before then."

Ron really liked the idea of having his mate there waiting for him. To his pleasure, Miles grunted as he tipped his head in a nod.

Almost thirty minutes later, Ron walked into the sheriff's office, whistling happily. He cut off his tune when he spotted Michelle—the office's ex-secretary and dispatcher—sitting at a desk talking with Deputy Nathan Kaldwell. The man was the only human left on Stone Ridge's police force, and Ron had no idea if the guy knew it or not. Either way, he'd always been a damn good deputy.

Crossing the office area, Ron headed for Sheriff Anthony Holsteen's office. The poison dart frog shifter was a new arrival and had fired Michelle first thing when she'd rattled off a number of slurs. It helped that there had been plenty of complaints against her.

Ron couldn't help his curiosity. "Hey, Sheriff," he greeted as he stepped into Anthony's office.

"Hi, Ron," Anthony replied without bothering to look at him. A second later, he snapped his head up. "Your scent's changed."

Grinning broadly, Ron quickly shut the door. "Yeah. Met your man's friend, Miles, while out running today," he told the sheriff, referring to Crew Kester—Anthony's mate who was also a member of Miles's team. "He's my mate."

Anthony grinned broadly, straightening in his chair. "Well, damn, Ron. Congratulations."

Even as Ron swelled with pride at being paired with such an amazing man, he couldn't help but ask, "Why is Michelle out there?" He sobered as he stated, "Please tell me she hasn't found a way to force you to rehire her."

Anthony scoffed as he shook his head. "That'll never happen," he vowed, sneering. Clearing his expression, Anthony told him, "No, she's here reporting a lost hiker. Her cousin, Baxter Winters."

Snorting upon hearing the man's name, Ron quipped, "Let me guess. He has thick, dark-brown hair, pale blue eyes stands six-foot-one, has a bit of a belly, and likes to wear camo pants and a black shirt."

To Ron's unease, he watched Anthony narrow his eyes as he slowly stood. "All correct except the clothing details. How did you know?"

Ron felt the blood drain from his face. "Oh shit."

CHAPTER FIVE

A fter giving Ron a kiss goodbye, Miles strode into the alpha's house. The fact that he wore only a pair of too-small
sweatpants wasn't what bothered him. Finding the front
room full of his team members caused a fissure of unease to
slither up his spine.

"Uh, hi, guys." Miles headed toward them, taking in their
various expressions. "I guess either Castrose or Prier shared
the news."

Miles's team leader, Bailey Dyer, rose to his feet. He was
mated with Clayton, Castrose's younger brother. Grinning,
he nodded as he held out his hand.

"Yeah," Bailey confirmed with a laugh. "Castrose spilled
the beans the second he walked into the workshop."

Bailey referred to the large workshop Beta Dixon had built
behind his home. As a bomb-maker, Clayton needed plenty
of space and privacy. Clayton and Bailey lived in a one-bed-
room apartment on the second floor.

Taking Miles's hand, he accepted his ex-team leader's
handshake and backslap. His cat rumbled happily in his
mind. They'd all been turned into cheetah shifters, but Bailey
hadn't lost his memory since he'd been saved by his brother,
Ronan, before the procedure could be completed. As it was,
their cheetahs thought of Bailey as the alpha of their mini
pride of cheetah shifters.

*Good thing, too, or we would have ended up murdering Bailey's
mate.*

Pushing that thought from his mind — *there isn't a damn*

thing I can do about the past—Miles released his friend's hand and nodded at the others. He noticed Warren and Nereo sat on a love seat positioned between the sofa occupied by David and Crew's chair. When Crew had begun the mating process with Anthony, David and Crew had had a falling out, when David had said some not-so-nice things out of jealousy, having been secretly infatuated with Crew for years. Even though David had found his own mate in a reclusive prepper named Brian, mending their friendship was still slow-going.

"So, ye're mated with Deputy Ron Reussmin," Alpha Declan commented as he strode into the room. The dark-skinned, Irish-born alpha wolf carried a tray holding a variety of drinks. "Congratulations." Grinning, flashing even white teeth, Declan added, "Are ye going to try to get on the force to work with him?"

"No," Miles immediately replied, shaking his head. He took a bottle of beer off the tray, then made his way to sit beside David on the large sofa. "I don't want anything that high-profile." Jerking his chin to indicate the others, Miles added, "Sure, we've turned General Sackett over to the CIA, but I still think there are people searching for us."

"The shadow operatives that attacked north of Brian's place gives testament to that," David agreed. Leaning forward, he took a beer, too, but he offered it to Crew first. After Crew had taken it, David took another and relaxed back on the sofa. "It sorta leaves a few of us twiddling our thumbs, though."

"I thought Brian's prepper set-up kept you busy," Nereo commented, grabbing beers for both him and Warren.

"It does," David confirmed.

Crew shrugged. "I'm renovating me and Anthony's cabin, so my hands are pretty full right now, too."

"I could use something to do," Bailey admitted, grabbing a brew for himself. "When Clayton gets lost in making a new bomb, he forgets, well . . . everything." Bailey's smile appeared fond, as if he found his mate's absentmindedness endearing.

"Well, Ron's home is already really nice," Miles commented, popping the cap on his drink. "So I'll need something to do while he's at work."

"Once we find a house and we move in, I probably will, too," Warren stated, rubbing the back of his neck. "Wow. All of us are mated to guys in the area. Weird to think about."

"That's Fate working her magick," Lark declared, striding into the room carrying a tray laden with finger sandwiches, chips, French onion dip, spear pickles, and sliced fruits. With a wide smile, he told them, "You're all family, so of course she'd want you all to be together." Sobering, Lark added, "Plus, with the report we just got from Agent Craigson about General Sackett, we all need to stick together."

Miles growled, irritation rising at the mention of his ex-stepfather. "Is that why we're all really here?"

"Afraid so." Declan made up a plate of food before heading to another small sofa. "There's pressure from another general"—he paused and glanced at something on his phone before continuing—"General Kitsom, trying to get the CIA to turn over General Sackett to the military police." Growling softly, Declan explained, "Saying something about it being their jurisdiction to charge him and investigate his crimes."

Anger churning within him, Miles clenched and released his jaw. He focused on something he could control and fixed himself a plate. Lark's egg salad sandwiches always tasted fantastic. Besides, Miles refused to allow that man's actions to affect him any longer.

I'm trying to anyway.

"How the hell did this General Kitsom even learn the CIA has Sackett?" Bailey asked on a growl.

Miles wondered the same thing and figured the others on the team were, too. It was just natural for their team leader to take the lead.

"Agent Craigson suspects either a leak or a hacker," Alpha Declan told them, shaking his head. "And so far, they're resisting under the claim that he's a threat to national security." Wincing, Declan admitted, "Prier is taking this as a personal challenge, so he intends to hack into the CIA database to see if anyone else has accessed it."

Lark settled next to Declan, curling against the alpha's side. "It's so good that the government is finally doing something about this crap."

Declan pecked a kiss to Lark's temple. "So they say." Then he returned his attention to them. "I'll keep ye all abreast of any new developments, but for now, I agree with yer idea of stayin' out of sight." Then his lips curved into a wide grin. "So, are we losing our last house guest soon?" Glancing toward Warren and Nereo, Declan added, "After the pair of ye find yer house, of course."

Taking the opening, Miles nodded as he quickly chewed his bite of food. "Yeah," he muttered before swallowing. Miles took a swig of his beer to wash it down, then stated, "I was wondering if I could borrow a vehicle. Ron gave me a key. I don't have a lot, but I'd like to have time to check his refrigerator and maybe go shopping if I need to."

"Do you plan to cook for him?" Lark grinned widely. "That's so sweet."

"No, it's not," Warren countered, smirking. "Miles can't cook."

Scowling at Warren, Miles growled softly. "I can manage a meal or two, asshole."

Warren tipped his head back and laughed, clearly unimpressed.

"So, you're moving in with him just like that?" Bailey sounded worried. "I didn't think you, uh, swung his way."

Clearing his throat, Miles realized he had to come clean. "I never mentioned how I got this." He pointed at the scar bisecting his left eyebrow. After seeing the guys exchange a look before they all shook their heads, Miles curled his lip as he shook his head. "Because it was too embarrassing." He swallowed hard before licking his lips. Even knowing none of them would hold it against him, he still hesitated. Finally, Miles admitted, "I thought a guy in a bar was checking me out, so I went and hit on him."

Bailey winced. "He wasn't checking you out?"

Miles shook his head. "There was a busty blonde sitting at a table to my left. That was why he kept looking my way." Rubbing the back of his neck, Miles continued, "Anyway, he and his friend took exception. A bar fight ensued. I won, but not before the friend managed to rake a broken bottle across my face." He rolled his eyes as he admitted, "Ended up in the hospital. Got twelve stitches, a scar, and a story I've never told anyone before." After another shrug, Miles admitted, "After that, I buried my bisexuality. Just seemed easier than trying to figure it out since I obviously missed out on that mystical gaydar."

"Even after Bailey and I came out to you as bisexual?" Warren murmured, sounding a little hurt. "Why?"

Miles shrugged again. "By then, it'd been over six years since that night. I had a good time with women." He shook his head. "I didn't see the point in unburying all that, so I let it go." Setting aside his half-full plate, Miles leaned forward and cradled his beer bottle between his knees. "Now though"—he glanced around at the guys who were essentially his family, seeing as his mother had died five years before—probably a good thing, all things considered—"I'm gonna need to talk to a couple of you about how to take care of a male lover."

"If ye don't mind me asking," Declan cut in softly. "Why didn't ye ask Ron?" Cocking his head, the alpha continued,

"Or did ye run out of time?"

"Trust issues," Miles revealed bluntly. He waved one hand, indicating the guys around him. "I trust these guys. Trust them to help me. Give it to me straight."

Lark snickered. "Or not so straight."

Miles smirked at the small blond. "Right." Upon seeing the twitch of Declan's lips, he added, "So, I bit Ron, starting our bond, but told him I needed to talk to you guys before doing more."

Declan straightened. "Ye bit Ron? Already?"

Nodding, Miles wondered at the alpha's surprise.

"Did he bite you, too?" Warren asked curiously.

Miles shook his head. "Was he supposed to?"

His cat grumbled in his mind, clearly thinking they'd missed out on something.

"Oh, you're so missing out," Crew muttered, staring hard at the floor, confirming Miles's cat's concern. "A claiming bite feels amazing."

Frowning, Miles muttered, "I wonder why Ron didn't bite me when I bit him."

"He may not have been expecting it," Declan pointed out. Before biting his sandwich in half, he asked, "Did ye discuss it beforehand?"

Miles shook his head again as he straightened in his seat. Thinking of their brief time together, he mused, "No. I'd explained that I wasn't rejecting him, that I wanted to be his partner, but I needed time with the fucking part of it." Hearing David snort, he explained, "I wanted to be forthcoming, and I'm a pretty blunt guy." Meeting Declan's smirking visage, Miles added, "I knew that claiming is important to shifters, and my cat was all for it, so when we were enjoying each other in the shower, I bit him."

Miles glanced around, noticing a couple of smirks, a flush on David's face, and how Crew was still staring at the floor.

Huh. I might have been too open there.

While the guys had ragged on each other when out picking up tricks, they didn't usually discuss details.

Recalling what had happened after biting Ron, Miles hummed before murmuring, "He did pass out, so maybe that's why." He rubbed at his own shoulder. "I'll have to talk to him about doing that to me."

"So, ye've started yer bond," Declan cut in, his dark lips twitching, his mirth apparent. "Congratulations again. Ye can borrow one of the pack trucks."

Miles knew there were three vehicles in various people's names that were available for general pack use—two trucks and an SUV.

"Thank you, Alpha," Miles replied, dipping his head in acknowledgment. Mentally shifting gears, he asked, "What happened with the asshole who snagged Ron? Is he talking?"

Alpha Declan rubbed a hand over his jaw, his eyes narrowing. "Castrose told me that he knew who Ron was in wolf form." His tone took on an annoyed growl. "He's currently with him and Prier. They're . . . chatting with him."

Lark sighed deeply. "I know what they're doing. You can use the word *interrogating*." Grimacing, he mumbled, "I'm the one who's going to have to bandage him up when they're done."

"I would have been happy to help," Nereo stated, a scowl creasing his features. "Then, no broken fingers."

"I appreciate the offer, Nereo. I really do." Alpha Declan focused on the vampire. Tapping the side of his head, he stated, "But I didn't feel it was right to keep using yer talents when it leaves ye with too many memories."

Nereo grinned broadly even as he shook his head. "That's a lovely sentiment, Alpha." Then he chuckled softly before saying, "But have no fear of that. It's just a part of a vampire's way of life. One of the first things we learn after going through puberty and transitioning into needing to drink blood, is the need for compartmentalization." As Nereo picked up a dill pickle spear, he stated, "Once you're comfortable considering me as part of your pack, I'd be honored if you used my skills."

Alpha Declan scoffed softly. "I understand what ye're saying, Nereo." Tapping his forefinger on his bottle, he gave the vampire an assessing look. "I suppose if I consider Lyle, Grady, and Gordon as part of my pack, I should think of ye the same way."

Miles knew the alpha referred to an altered monitor lizard shifter, a Bengal tiger shifter, and an elephant shifter, respectively. While not wolves, they were still considered members of Alpha Declan's pack. From what Miles had learned over the last few months, the alpha had adopted a number of shifters into his pack.

What's a vampire, then?

Alpha Declan's phone ringing interrupted the conversation. He pulled it from his pocket and answered.

Miles focused on eating, feeding his large shifter appetite. He'd finished off another sandwich and was enjoying some chips and dip when Alpha Declan's growl caught his attention. Snapping his head up, Miles focused on the wolf shifter, taking in his narrowed gray eyes and stormy expression as he disconnected the call.

"Was that about Ron's would-be kidnapper?" Miles asked, needing to know if his wolf was in any further danger.

"No," Declan replied, surprising him. "That was Sheriff Anthony." Pinning Miles with a serious gaze, he told him, "Evidently, the man we have in custody is Baxter Winters. He's Michelle Laraby's cousin, and she's reporting him as a lost hiker." With a sneer, Declan added, "As the head park ranger in this area, I'm being charged with conducting a search and rescue for the asshole."

Lark gaped up at him. "What are you going to do?"

Declan focused on Nereo. "It looks like I'm going to need

yer help after all."

Miles glanced between them before declaring, "I want to go, too."

After a second of eyeing him, as if trying to decide on his intentions, Alpha Declan nodded. "Very well, seeing as he attacked yer mate." He smiled, adding, "Even if ye didn't know it at the time."

"Thank you, Alpha." Miles rose, grabbing one more sandwich to go. "I'll go get dressed."

Chapter Six

When Ron walked out of Sheriff Anthony's office, he glanced Michelle's way. He saw her eyes widen just a little, as if she was surprised to see him there. Ron made a mental note to share that with the sheriff after she'd left.

Ron headed into the back and clocked in before checking his schedule. After seeing he had dispatch duty nearly halfway through his shift, he grabbed the keys to one of the department's two patrol cruisers. He nodded to Nathan, who was still talking to Michelle, and headed out on patrol.

When Anthony had taken over as sheriff and fired Michelle, he'd offered the position to Nereo. The vampire had counter-offered by accepting a deputy position if he wasn't the only one who worked the phones. Anthony had agreed, and now all the deputies took a turn manning them. That way, no one ended up stuck behind a desk all the time.

While it was normally boring as hell, Ron thought the change was a good idea.

Three hours later, after having looked into one car accident, a downed power line, and a report about a fire, which had ended up being someone burning trash in a barrel, Ron returned to the office to take his turn on the phones.

Seeing his brother Markus behind the desk, Ron grinned at him.

Markus scowled back.

Pausing beside the desk, Ron cocked his head. "Who burned your toast?" he asked, wondering about his brother's mood.

Rising slowly, Markus held Ron's gaze. Instead of answering, he reached up. Crooking a finger, he slid it under Ron's shirt collar and pulled it aside, revealing the very lovely claiming scar Miles had given him. Markus glanced at it pointedly, before arching one brow in silent question.

Ron felt heat on his neck and cheeks as he tried valiantly to squelch an embarrassed blush.

Right. Should have called him.

"Um, sorry," Ron muttered, easing back a step, causing Markus to release his shirt. "I should have called to tell you."

Markus smirked as he chuckled, his expression relaxing. "After the grief you gave me when I told our alpha about meeting Ronan first and not you." His brother shook his head as he rolled his eyes. "Had to give you a little shit."

Then Markus opened his arms and grabbed Ron in a bear hug. "Congratulations, brother."

Ron returned the hug, holding his brother tightly. "Thanks, Markus. I *am* sorry I forgot to call." When Markus eased his hold, Ron held his gaze. "I just . . ." He scoffed. "I don't know. Was a crazy morning."

"I can understand that," Markus conceded, releasing him to lean a hip against the desk. "Meeting your mate can sort of scramble your brain. Makes you do stuff out of character." With a wink, he finished, "Like forgetting to call your brother . . . or your alpha . . . about the news?"

Feeling the blood drain from his face, Ron whispered, "Oh shit."

Markus tipped his head back and laughed. He slapped Ron on the upper arm. "He knows. Castrose told him," he assured. "Besides, Miles lives with him."

Blowing out a relieved breath, Ron wiped the back of his hand over his forehead in a dramatic fashion. "Whew."

Sobering, Markus asked, "So what's this about a trap?"

As Ron moved behind the desk, taking over for Markus,

who must have relieved Nathan, he explained his morning's misadventure.

Growling, Markus glared at him. "You went running without telling anyone?" He glanced toward the front of the building, but the doors remained closed. Lowering his voice, Markus hissed, "What the hell were you thinking?"

"Guess I wasn't," Ron admitted, his shoulders sagging. "Just wanted to stretch my legs before coming in to work." He frowned as he shook his head. "I didn't even go that far from my house. Just fifteen minutes or so."

"At least it worked out." Markus rested his hand on Ron's shoulder and squeezed, clearly relieved. "Having a responsible mate to look after you will be good for you."

Ron scowled at Markus. "Ha ha."

Markus grimaced. "I didn't mean it like that. I just—"

The phone rang, and Ron picked it up. "Stone Ridge sheriff's office."

"So you got away," an electronically altered voice snarled through the line. "It won't be for long. Better watch your back, abomination, because I won't stop until I get my due."

Before Ron could even hope to come up with a response, the caller hung up.

"Okaaaaaay." Markus drew the word out, revealing that he'd overheard.

Ron peered up at his brother. "Well, we know Baxter has an accomplice."

Markus nodded. "Someone who thinks shifters owe him."

Nodding, Ron shared his suspicions of Michelle. "She sure looked surprised to see me."

"She'd be the obvious suspect," Markus mused, scowling at the floor.

"Everything okay?" Sheriff Anthony asked, striding toward them. "Why the pensive looks? I'd think you'd be happier right now."

Even as the thought of his mate lifted Ron's spirits, pulling a smile to his lips, he still worried over the phone call. He listened as Markus explained the call to their boss. Ron felt grateful for his older brother's reassuring hand on his shoulder.

"So, someone's coming after a shifter as payback for something," Sheriff Anthony grumbled, crossing his arms over his slender torso. The brown-haired man wasn't a big man by any means, only standing at five-foot-ten. His dominant personality, however, more than made up for his size. "I know you're thinking Michelle, just like I am, but we need to keep an open mind."

"Yes, sir," Ron immediately replied.

"Head out on patrol, Markus," Sheriff Anthony urged. "I'm going to report this to Alpha Declan." As he headed toward his office, he continued, "I think I recall him saying something about Prier or Raul monitoring our lines."

"Note to self," Ron mumbled. "No phone sex on the desk line."

Markus snorted as he smacked Ron upside the head. "Perv."

As Ron rubbed the back of his head, he watched his brother head out to start his patrol. He knew he would miss his brother when he was no longer a deputy. Due to his mate still being wanted by the military police, Markus intended to quit and remake his identity. The pair would hide out in the woods, relying on the pack for a decade to provide things that they couldn't grow or hunt themselves.

Anthony had convinced Markus to stick around for a few months while he hired a couple of more deputies. So far, the only addition had been Nereo. Even as Ron wanted his brother happy, he hoped it took the sheriff at least another month or two. Ron truly enjoyed working with his brother.

Oh well. Times change.

Ron grinned.

And I have my own mate to come home to now.

With that thought in mind, Ron tried to focus on work. He used his time at the front desk to write up his reports from the first few hours of his patrol. He couldn't help how often his mind drifted to Miles, however. The big, blond male was just sexy beyond all reason.

And he already bit me.

Ron couldn't wait for a chance to return the favor. He hoped his cheetah would be amendable to wearing his claiming scar. While Ron wasn't an exceptionally dominant shifter, he still wanted to mark his mate.

"Have a great night, Ron," Nathan called with a wave as he walked past the front desk. Then the human paused and stared hard at him. "There's something different about you." Before Ron could figure out how to respond to that, Nathan's eyes widened. A second later, his lips curved into a shit-eating grin. "I know that look." He pointed a finger at Ron's face. "I saw it on my older sister when she started dating her husband." Resting his hands on his hips, Nathan asked, "Who's the lucky girl?"

"Guy, actually," Ron replied automatically. "His name is Miles."

Nathan chuckled. "There must be something in the water here. It's like a gay mecca." With a shrug, he added, "I'd be worried if I weren't bisexual myself." After Nathan rapped his knuckles on the desk, he turned and started toward the door, calling, "Good for you, Ron. Can't wait to meet him."

Then Nathan was gone, leaving Ron in stunned silence.

Huh.

"That human is damn perceptive," Anthony stated with a shake of his head. After a tap on Ron's shoulder, he added, "I'm on dispatch next. You can head back out on patrol."

Even as Ron rose to his feet, he couldn't help gaping at Anthony. "You're taking a turn on the phones?"

"Sure," Anthony confirmed, settling in the chair and starting to adjust its height. When Ron didn't move, too surprised to get his feet unstuck from the floor, the sheriff looked up at him. He smirked as he tapped the desk. "You think just because I'm sheriff that I won't do this job?"

"Uhhh, sorry." Ron yanked his head out of his ass. "Just would never have seen Sheriff Parkinson taking a turn on the phones." Lifting his hands in placation, he quickly added, "And I know you're not him. Still getting used to it."

Smirking, Anthony pointed toward the doors. "Nope, I'm not him, and I take that as a compliment. Now off you go."

Ron nodded and quickly did as the more dominant shifter bid.

"Oh, Deputy?"

With his window rolled down so he could enjoy the fresh evening air, Ron easily made out the female call. He glanced in his rearview mirror and spotted Winona Phishmy waving on the sidewalk behind him. Ron stopped the cruiser, checked his rearview mirror again, then put his vehicle in reverse and carefully made his way back to her.

Ron hadn't received any calls, so he'd been patrolling the side streets, listening and scenting for trouble.

"Good evening, Misses Phishmy," Ron greeted the middle-aged brunette with a smile. "How can I help you?"

Winona pressed a hand to her chest as she told him, "I am so glad you happened by." She pointed upward with her other hand. "I know it's not really your thing, but I can't get Olive out of the tree. She got out of the house and raced right up before I could stop her."

Leaning over the passenger seat, Ron peered upward. He spotted a large calico cat on a tree branch about eighteen feet up. Fighting back a groan, he straightened in his seat.

As odd as it sounded, Ron would have preferred she told

51

him a guy was burglarizing her house. He would rather face down a man with a gun than a cat in a tree. As a wolf shifter, he didn't seem to get along with natural cats very well.

Oh well. Part of the job.

After radioing in that he would be away from his cruiser while giving the code for a cat in a tree, Ron stepped from his car. "Do you have a ladder, Misses Phishmy?"

"Um." Her brows furrowed. "Maybe in the shed out back?"

Ron nodded. "I'll hurry back and take a look." Starting that way, he asked, "Is it locked?"

Winona shook her head.

"Be right back." Ron hurried away, more than ready for his day to be over.

With several healing scratches on his arm and one on his neck, Ron climbed back into the cruiser. He grabbed a napkin out of the glove box, and while peering at his reflection in the sun visor mirror, he dabbed at his neck.

"Are you sure I can't interest you in a band-aid, Deputy?" Winona bent to peer in at him, putting the tops of her round tits on clear display. "I'd be happy to doctor your wounds."

Ron had caught the scent of the woman's arousal when he'd climbed off the ladder and handed over her cat. The smell had only been more intense when he'd returned from putting away her ladder. A glance over his shoulder had told him she had her attention pinned on his ass.

Evidently, Winona Phishmy had a thing for men's butts in uniform.

Just great.

"I'll really be fine, ma'am," Ron replied, needing to get away from her before his bleeding stopped, making her suspicious. "I've had plenty worse."

Ron just didn't want to get blood on his uniform collar. That would be a bitch to get out. Firing up his cruiser, he waved and urged, "Best get that kitty of yours in the house. Be careful she doesn't get out again."

"Of course, Deputy." Her expression and scent screamed disappointment. "Thanks again, and take care now."

After another wave, Ron put the car in gear and started on his way. He'd just begun to round the corner, preparing to turn onto a bridge built over a creek that fed a larger river, when the roar of an engine reached his ears. Ron snapped his attention to the right and gaped, freezing for an instant.

A large dark-colored pick-up with tinted windows was barreling toward him from a side street.

Ron slammed his foot on the accelerator, making the tires spin for an instant before catching on the asphalt. Rocketing forward, he swerved left, trying to avoid being hit. A hard jolt told Ron that he hadn't succeeded.

His car slid to the left toward the guardrail. The truck kept pushing, causing metal to squeal under the onslaught. Gripping the wheel tightly, Ron braced.

Except, instead of the guardrail stopping them, Ron's car's tire must have hit it just right. His front end popped up, giving him a clear view of the stars above. A second later, he pitched forward again, and Ron's cruiser tumbled into the ravine.

CHAPTER SEVEN

M iles was exiting the grocery store when his cell phone
began to ring. Considering it was a burner phone that
he'd been given by Alpha Declan—the alpha had provided
one to each of his team—he knew few people had the number.
That meant it was most likely important.

Stopping on the sidewalk, Miles placed the two bags he'd
been carrying in his right hand onto the ground. He pulled
the small phone from his back pocket. Miles saw Crew's name
and wondered what he could want.

Certainly not to talk about anal sex.

As it had turned out, Crew had been the only real straight
guy in their unit. When Fate had mated him with a man, he'd
tried to run and deny. Not surprisingly, that hadn't worked
out so well for him.

Crew had ended up having a very discreet conversation
with their team leader, Bailey. Neither man revealed what
they'd talked about. From his behavior earlier that day, Miles
figured gay sex talk was still hard for him.

Instead, Miles had spent a very informative half-hour with
Warren and Bailey. That had been after returning with Alpha
Declan and Nereo—after the vampire had extracted every bit
of pertinent information from Baxter's brain. Too bad there
hadn't been that much of it.

So what could he possibly want?

With only one way to find out, Miles answered the call.
"Yes?"

Miles knew that Crew would be able to recognize his voice.

"You still in town?" Crew was just as direct and to the point.

"I am."

"I'm texting you an address," Crew told him. "Go there. Ron was in an accident."

Hissing, Miles scowled at the ground. "What kind of accident?" He scooped up the bags on the ground, carrying all four in his left hand, and started toward his borrowed truck.

"Anthony called me. Someone ran his cruiser off the road," Crew told him. "That's all I know."

"Thanks," Miles replied swiftly. "Send me the address."

Miles disconnected the call, shoved his phone in his pocket, and drew out his keys. After hitting the fob to unlock it, he slid it between his teeth to hold it. He opened the back door, tossed his bags uncaringly onto the floor, and moved to the front.

Taking his keys from his mouth and his phone from his pocket, Miles climbed behind the wheel. By the time he fired up the engine, he had a text from Crew. Miles quickly punched the address into the truck's GPS system, then followed its directions.

As Miles drove, he wondered if this could be related in any way to Ron being caught in wolf form earlier in the day. If it was, he had to accept that someone had a serious hard-on for his mate.

And not the good kind.

Unfortunately, Baxter hadn't been able to tell them anything about who had given him the information necessary to set the pig snare. Everything had been sent to Baxter from a burner phone. When Prier had tried to ping the phone, nothing had happened, telling them that it was off.

Prier had assured Miles and Declan that he would keep monitoring it.

The files on Baxter's phone had given not just Ron's address, but also an aerial map. There had been pictures of Ron in human and wolf form. The aerial map even had prospective running routes marked upon it. Plus, there had been detailed instructions on how to handle and set several different types of traps, all while never putting a human scent on them.

Someone has some serious hunting experience.

Miles spotted flashing lights as soon as he turned onto the road. A police cruiser was parked fifty feet away, and a barricade had been set up. Someone in uniform that Miles didn't know was directing traffic.

Easing to the side of the road, Miles parked the truck. He swung out, shut and locked the door, then began jogging toward the stranger. Even before Miles reached him, the guy was holding up his hand, palm out, and resting his hand on his holstered sidearm.

Not wanting to get shot, Miles slowed his approach. He held his hands wide, palms forward.

"I'm sorry, sir," the human stated firmly. "This is an active crime scene. I'm going to need you to get back in your truck and turn around." He pointed back the way Miles had come. "You can get to Pagodi Street via Vine or Madison."

"My name is Miles." He hesitated, realizing he needed to keep his last name out of any records. Still, he wasn't leaving until he found out what the hell was going on. "Sheriff Anthony called his partner, Crew," Miles started again, name dropping in hopes that it helped. "Crew called me. I'm Ron's boyfriend. I heard he was in an accident, and I was already in town."

"Miles?" The human's brows furrowed, seeming to recognize the name.

Miles nodded even as he wondered if Ron had mentioned him to his co-workers already, and he found the idea warmed his gut a little. The sensation even chased away some of the chill he'd been dealing with ever since hearing that Ron had been driven off the road.

"Please stand there," Nathan ordered, pointing for Miles to

stay. Then he reached up and pressed the side button on the microphone attached to his shoulder. "Sheriff? I have a Miles here who says he's connected with Ron."

"Send him back, Deputy Nathan," Anthony immediately ordered.

The human, Deputy Nathan, seemed surprised by that, and his brows shot up. Still, he responded in the affirmative. Then he pointed toward the accident, saying, "Go ahead."

Miles immediately picked up a jog and sped past Nathan. The hairs on his nape standing on end told him the human most likely watched, but he ignored it. Instead, he swept his gaze over the area, searching for a wrecked cruiser, an ambulance, or even a fire truck.

He didn't spot the first two, but a fire truck was parked on the very right side just before where the road traversed onto a bridge.

As Miles drew closer, he spotted where the guardrail had been torn away, and his stomach flipped uncomfortably.

Oh, god.

Ropes were attached to hooks on the side of the fire truck, and several people were being lowered into the ravine.

"Miles."

He recognized Anthony's voice, but he couldn't rip his gaze away from the scene as he drew to the side of the bridge. Looking down, he felt his heart lodge in his throat. Twenty feet below, leaning precariously against several trees, was a beat-up cruiser.

Miles had seen so much destruction while overseas, but nothing could have prepared him for seeing his wolf shifter mate's car hanging dangerously in some trees. One wrong stiff breeze could send the vehicle sliding even farther into the crevasse, making it fall at least another twenty feet.

"Take a deep breath, Miles." Anthony rested a hand on his shoulder, squeezing lightly and drawing his attention to the shorter man. The sheriff's voice was low as he stated, "Byron and Paolo are the ones being lowered down. They're shifters. They'll get Ron out of there safely."

After taking several deep, slow breaths, Miles managed to tear his attention away from the damaged car far below him. "What happened?" he asked, focusing on Anthony.

The frog shifter's pale-green eyes narrowed, and his lips pinched for a few seconds. "Ron had just finished helping a civilian, and he was heading out of the neighborhood," he explained. "She watched a big black truck speed out of a side road. According to her, it was doing way over the speed limit, ignored the stop sign, and slammed into Ron's back end. After his car flipped over the side, it headed out of sight." With a shake of his head, he muttered, "She thought drunk driver."

"But that's not what you think." Miles caught on quickly enough.

Anthony shook his head. "Not after the phone call at the precinct."

Frowning, Miles asked, "What phone call?"

After hearing about the phone threat, Miles growled softly under his breath. "Just who the hell has Ron in his crosshairs?"

"Don't know," Anthony admitted. "But we'll figure it out."

Hell yeah, I will.

Miles didn't bother replying, too busy staring into the ravine. He noted that the pair seemed to be talking to Ron, which meant he was conscious. He decided that was something, at least.

My mate is lucid. He'll be fine.

As Miles watched, the larger guy — Byron, a wolf shifter, according to Anthony — gripped the frame of the sedan under a wheel well, obviously holding it steady. He nodded at Paolo — a rat shifter. Paolo gripped the door handle in both hands, planted his feet, and pulled. Even from on the bridge, Miles could see the other shifter's muscles straining.

Finally, with an almighty groan, Paolo managed to ease the

door halfway open.

The car wobbled in the trees.

Byron snapped something, and Paolo made quick work of reaching in and dragging Ron from the car.

That was when Miles spotted Markus. Ron's brother was being lowered in another harness, guiding a backboard that was being lowered beside him. He was talking, but hell if Miles could make out what he was saying.

Still, Miles recognized the lines around Markus's mouth. The wolf shifter was worried as hell.

"Uh, Sheriff?" Nathan's voice came through his microphone.

"Go ahead, Deputy Nathan," Anthony replied.

"Now I have a Doctor Lark Trystan here." The human sounded dubious. "He says he's Ron's primary physician, but he's not here in an ambulance."

"Let him and his ride pass," Anthony ordered. Closing his eyes, he tipped his head back to stare at the heavens. "The write-up on this is going to be a nightmare."

Miles growled, glaring at the frog shifter. "Is *that* what you're worried about here?" he snarled. "Paperwork?"

Anthony snapped his eyes open and gave Miles a quelling look. "Of course not," he replied harshly. "But I have faith that our people will take good care of Ron, so I have to look at the bigger picture." Tugging his work hat from his head, Anthony grumbled, "Namely, how to make it so we don't get investigated by outside forces."

"Sorry," Miles forced himself to say. Rubbing the tips of his forefingers over the scar bisecting his brow, he admitted, "I'm sort of known as the blunt asshole of our team."

Scoffing, Anthony patted him on the back. "You're in good company then." He tipped his chin toward a pack SUV that was weaving closer. "Why don't you go wait with the doc? I'm sure you plan to stick close to Ron's side."

Miles nodded and took a couple of steps away from the sheriff. Turning, he dug into his pocket and pulled out his truck's keys. "It's the pack's." Then he winced and added, "There's ice cream in the back along with some other stuff."

"I'll take care of it," Anthony assured, taking the keys. He made a shooing gesture with his other hand. "I'll be there to check with them shortly." Then the sheriff pulled up his phone and put in a call to Fire Chief Brahms—according to the tag on his phone, anyway.

Dismissing Anthony, Miles swept his gaze over the scene once more. He spotted where the pack SUV had finally parked. Seeing Lark and Declan at the back, pulling out a gurney, Miles jogged in their direction.

"Can I give you all a hand?" Miles asked, announcing himself.

Lark offered Miles a tight smile while Declan gripped his shoulder briefly.

"We may need your help getting him loaded on here," Lark told him as he started toward where Ron was still being cranked up to the fire truck. Lark nearly whispered his next words as they were getting close to a number of others. "And I know his wolf will be more settled with you by his side."

The human working the winch tipped his chin. "Guys. I'll have Ron and Markus up in just another minute."

"We appreciate it, Stake," Declan replied, proving that he knew the man. Then the wolf alpha headed closer to the ledge and a man who seemed to be overseeing everything. "Got a preliminary, Brahms?"

That must be the fire chief.

Miles helped Lark maneuver the gurney closer.

"Broken left arm. Concussion. Couple of cracked or broken ribs." Brahms grimaced as he met the alpha's gaze. "A puncture in the upper gastric area and multiple fractures to his right leg." The shifter actually appeared to pale. "Ron's got bones sticking out, so Doc will have his work cut out for him."

"Shit," Miles hissed, feeling his stomach lurch, threatening to expel the light supper he'd eaten not that long before.

Brahms turned his way, and his eyes narrowed. "You his . . . partner?" The shifter seemed to catch himself just in time.

Miles nodded. "I am." Before Brahms could reply, he quickly added, "He'll be well taken care of as he mends."

And he will mend. I refuse to consider any other outcome.

After jerking a nod, Brahms turned his attention to Lark. "We're going to swing Ron over here." He indicated a cleared area. "Let's get this set up."

Within just a couple of minutes, Markus and Ron appeared over the edge. "Doc!" Markus called.

"Here." Lark began reaching for the harness holding Ron to the backboard. "Let's get him over here." Lowering his voice once more, he muttered, "You give him the meds?"

"Yeah, and he's out," Markus replied, just as quietly. He grimaced before admitting, "But he was about to pass out from pain anyway."

Miles noticed Ron's slack jaw and shallow breaths, telling him that, while he was unconscious, he was still in pain.

Shaking his head, Miles followed Lark's instructions to the T as he helped the doc and Declan move Ron's lax body to the gurney. While Ron didn't wake, he did moan piteously. The sound went straight to Miles's heart, and anger surged through him. He wanted to track down whoever had dared to do this to his mate, and he had every intention of shredding him limb from limb.

"Relax, Miles," Alpha Declan crooned into his ear. "Let's get out of here. We'll find the culprits later." Then he squeezed the back of Miles's neck before pushing him gently toward the SUV. "Get in the back. You can help me load from inside."

Miles followed the alpha wolf's instructions, helping get

Ron's gurney locked into place in the back. Taking a seat near his mate's head, he folded Ron's slack hand between both of his own. Then Miles focused on keeping himself calm as Declan headed back to the lodge.

So much for our first night together.

But we'll have more.

Many more.

Miles would accept no less.

CHAPTER EIGHT

A persistent and annoying *beep, beep, beep* slowly tugged Ron to consciousness. He twitched the fingers of his right hand, wanting to shut off the blasted alarm. When his arm didn't immediately obey, Ron struggled to rouse more fully.

Except, his brain felt cloudy . . . fuzzy . . . and he was having trouble focusing.

Why do I feel like this?

Ron could only recall one time feeling so out of it. That had been when someone had slipped a roofie into his drink at a club. He'd certainly learned his lesson about never leaving his drink unattended that night.

Fortunately, Markus had been there. He'd recognized the odd signs, and he'd stuck by Ron until he'd begun to think more clearly. Due to Ron's shifter metabolism, it had only taken about fifteen minutes. They'd even managed to get the guy arrested, so he could never do it to anyone else ever again. Ron and Markus had woven a tale about how he hadn't ingested the full dose, which had allowed him to realize what was going on.

Except, I haven't been to a club in over a decade. And I certainly have never drank enough to feel like this. What the hell is going on?

Finally, the warmth cradling Ron's right hand registered. He twitched his fingers again, feeling the slight scrape of callouses against his fingertips. The sensation caused the hairs on his arm to stand on end, filling him with new sensations.

Nice.

"Come on, Ron," a deep voice crooned into his ear. "I know

you're coming out of it. Let me see those gorgeous hazel eyes."

Ron struggled to recognize the voice.

Then it hit him.

My mate. And he sounds worried.

Fighting hard to open his eyes, Ron worked to obey Miles's urgings. He felt his eyelids flutter, and he groaned in frustration. He tried harder and managed to open them a sliver.

To Ron's relief, only dim lighting greeted him, but everything seemed blurry. Blinking a few times, he managed to open his eyes wider with each pass. It took longer than Ron would have wished, or even thought possible, but finally, he could make out the room's features.

I'm in the lodge . . . in one of Lark's medical suites. What the hell?

Just that fast, it all came rushing back—the cat in the tree, the truck, the bridge . . . even Byron and Paolo pulling him from his precariously perched sedan.

Ron remembered the pain. It had been more intense than anything he could ever remember experiencing. Even getting shot twice while in the line of duty hadn't given him the whole-body agony that the accident had.

Of course, Ron remembered most of it had been centered in his right leg. Between the blood and bone sticking out of his ruined pants' leg, he'd known it'd been broken in several places. Ending up at Alpha Declan's in Lark's infirmary made sense.

"Come on, pretty wolf," Miles encouraged again. "Focus those lovely hazel eyes and look at me."

Ron felt a gentle touch to his jaw. "I'm focused," he tried to say, but his words came out strangely garbled. Instead, Ron groaned and allowed his eyelids to slide closed again.

"My poor mate," Miles purred into his ear before pressing a light kiss to his temple. "Got someone after you, but we'll figure it out." He bussed another kiss to Ron's temple. "I'll keep you safe. You have my word."

After a couple of slow deep breaths, Ron forced his eyelids open again. It was easier that time. He stared at the ceiling for a heartbeat, then two, before carefully turning his attention to the right.

Seeing Miles's paler than normal skin and drawn, worried features, Ron wanted to kick his own ass for worrying his cheetah so much. Except, he knew it wasn't his fault, not really. He'd been intentionally rammed.

Ron opened his mouth, and Miles touched his chin. "Just a sec," his mate murmured. Miles quickly released his hand as he straightened out of Ron's view. Ron wanted to protest, but Miles was back an instant later, holding a cup with a bendy straw in it. "Drink . . . slowly."

Then Miles slipped the end of the straw into Ron's mouth.

Obeying, Ron sipped carefully. The first half-mouthful of cool water drew a whimper from him as it slid down his throat. It felt and tasted that good.

Ron quickly sucked a larger mouthful and swallowed it, followed by a third. As he was drawing in a fourth, Miles eased the straw from his mouth.

When Ron moaned his protest, Miles shushed him, his expression pained. "I want to give you all you want so badly," his mate admitted. "But doctor's orders." Placing the cup somewhere out of sight near Ron's head—maybe a nightstand—Miles continued, "I hit the button to call Lark, so I'm sure he'll be here soon." Petting lightly through Ron's hair, Miles told him, "He hasn't left the house since you were brought in. That was night before last."

Damn. A day and a half.

Ron finally noticed the slight bags under Miles's eyes. He could just guess that his mate hadn't gotten much sleep during that time. Just as he was thinking about forcing his throat to work, the door opened.

Lark entered first, followed by Markus. Declan and Raul

came next. The human hacker had a tablet in hand. Ronan remained in the doorway. The big marine crossed his arms over his chest as he leaned one shoulder against the doorframe. He offered Ron an encouraging smile before he cast a worried gaze Markus's way.

Yup. My brother has bags under his eyes, too.

Shit.

"Sorry," Ron managed to force out.

"Hey," Miles stated on a growl. "There's nothing for you to be sorry for. This wasn't your fault."

Ron blinked, struggling with his memories. He distinctly recalled freezing in shock for a few seconds. If he'd reacted immediately, maybe he —

"Ron, Miles is right." Markus stood at Miles's side, staring at him with brotherly love in his eyes. "You're being targeted." Then Markus exchanged a look with Miles before refocusing on Ron. "We're just trying to figure out who and why."

"Other than ye being a shifter, of course," Alpha Declan cut in, sweeping a concerned gaze over his prone form. "No other shifters have been attacked while ye've been here."

"Making us believe that whoever it is has a bone to pick with you," Raul cut in, barely glancing up from whatever he was doing on his tablet. "Either that or they know that a few of you are shifters but don't feel comfortable going after others, yet." Scoffing, Raul muttered, "From Baxter's own words and memories, he was in contact with someone who knows who the leader is." He paused long enough to point a finger at Declan. "And I'd imagine they know that Markus is a shifter, too, but he lives quite a bit higher up the mountain than Ron does." Finally, Raul lifted his gaze and focused on Ron with a frown. "You're close to town and a likable guy." He lifted his free hand in placation. "There's nothing wrong with that, but it means just about everyone knows you."

"I'm an easy target," Ron mumbled.

"Eh." Raul shrugged before nodding. Then he refocused on his tablet. "So, what do you remember about your accident?"

"Can't this wait?" Lark grumbled. As Raul had been talking, the doc had been busy checking his IV, as well as the machine he was hooked up to. "I'd like to check over my patient. If this gets Ron worked up—"

"It's okay," Ron insisted roughly. He turned his attention back to Miles. "Water?"

After focusing on Lark, who gave him a quick nod, Miles brought the straw back to his lips.

Ron drank gratefully, although slowly. After three gulps, he turned his head while using his tongue to push the straw from his mouth. Then he looked toward his mate while turning his right hand over.

Miles immediately caught on and threaded his fingers with Ron's own.

Drawing comfort from his mate's touch, Ron admitted, "I remember everything . . . about that day." He focused on Raul. "I want to help."

Raul nodded once, a smile on his lips. "Glad to hear it, Ron." Holding his gaze, the human added, "I'm also glad to see you on the mend." After Ron nodded a little, Raul refocused on his table. "Okay. Down to business." He met Ron's gaze and asked, "Do you know the make, model, color, and license plate number of the truck that hit you?" Grimacing, Raul revealed, "All Winona could tell us was that it was dark and it was a pick-up truck. She called it black, but"—he shrugged—"it was dark."

Letting out a soft breath, Ron recalled those few horrifying seconds that were etched into his brain. "Older model *Ford.* Black with blue accents. Rust around the wheel wells." Licking his lips, he blinked a couple of times. "Tinted windows, but whoever was behind the wheel had a big frame. Definitely male."

"That rules our Michelle as our motorist," Markus muttered, frowning. "Damn."

Ron grimaced as he nodded at his brother. Returning his attention to Raul, he whispered, "First four numbers of the plate are niner-vincent-zulu-zero." Shaking his head, he muttered, "I didn't catch the rest before I was bracing for impact."

Raul grinned at him. "Still. Impressive. Okay . . . oh." He frowned as he grunted softly. "That plate is registered to a nineteen-ninety-eight *Ford*. It's owned by retired Sheriff Blake Parkinson."

"I thought Blake moved to some town in Wyoming?" Alpha Declan questioned. "Near his sister?"

Nodding slowly, Raul muttered, "Yeah. Jared confirmed it with traffic cameras." He winced. "Uh, Prier." Shaking his head, he grumbled, "Not sure I'll get used to that. Fifteen years calling him by one name, and I'm just supposed to forget in a matter of months."

Alpha Declan chuckled. "He's finding he doesn't much like the name, either."

Raul snorted. "Yeah, he had Jared added to his new identity as a middle name. Guess it'll be fine either way. Hey, wait." Raul fell silent as he scowled and poked at his tablet.

At least focusing on the pair allowed Ron to ignore the check-up Lark was putting him through. The way he pressed on certain areas of his chest and torso hurt like hell. He grimaced here and there but managed to keep his mouth shut.

"Okay. Sooooo." Raul lifted his attention and met Declan's gaze. "There's a bill of sale being processed by our county government. This truck's title is being transferred into the name of Lukas Roma, but a preliminary search brings up nothing on the guy." Shaking his head, Raul turned toward the door. "I need to get to some more powerful equipment and collaborate with Jared." As Raul disappeared out the door, he called, "I'll get back to you as soon as I have some-thing."

Declan shrugged after Raul had gone. "Does a Lukas Roma ring a bell with anyone?"

Ron shook his head just a smidge, while everyone else was a little more vibrant about it.

"Okay." Lark squeezed Ron's shoulder and offered him a smile. "So, you ready for the good news or the bad news?"

"Let me guess," Ron murmured, forcing a smile. "The good news is that I'm alive?"

Lark snorted as he smiled at him. "Yeah, but that's not the *only* good news." Setting down his clipboard, he hooked a rolling stool with his foot and dragged it close. Once Lark had settled on it, he rested his forearms on his thighs while smil-ing at Ron. "So, no broken ribs. Just cracks in three of them, and they're well on their way to being mended."

"Explains why it's easier to breathe."

Ron recalled having to focus on taking slow, shallow breaths. In truth, he'd felt damn grateful that his radio had still worked after his accident. Staring through a window at the small river winding along the gorge below, Ron had been worried no one would reach him in time . . . or would be able to get him out.

Thank the gods for shifter strength.

"Gonna have to send a gift basket to Paolo and a few oth-ers," Ron mumbled absently.

"I already did," Miles told him, an enigmatic smile curving his lips. "I had a fun time shopping for flavored lube. It'll be even more fun to do it together." With a wink, Miles asked, "Perhaps you'd like a pair of fuzzy handcuffs."

Recalling that Paolo was into leather and bondage, Ron groaned and shook his head. "Not for me."

"That's fine." Miles rubbed over Ron's upper arm sooth-ingly. "I've cuffed enough bad guys to never feel the need to do it to my lover."

"Well, that's more than I wanted to know about you two," Markus drawled, staring at the ceiling.

"How about I finish with the good news, bad news?" Lark quipped, trying to hide his mirth.

"Sounds like a plan." Ron didn't talk a whole lot with Markus about their sex lives . . . beyond safety and being careful and such. Of course, those talks were well behind them. Focusing on Lark, he asked, "So, how long am I laid up?"

"Good news, your concussion will have cleared by now," Lark told him, holding his gaze. He pointed at Ron's belly. "The piece of glass embedded in your abdomen ended up being shallow, and it missed all your organs. Another two days, and you probably won't even have a scar." Then Lark's expression grew serious. "Your arm was a clean break, so only another week and a half, probably, as long as you take it easy."

Ron thought all that sounded good, considering the severity of the accident. "Okay." He let out a deep breath. "The bad news?"

Lark grimaced. "Your right leg's tibia ended up in three pieces. I did surgery and put a plate in to hold the bones together. Once you're almost healed, I'll need to do another surgery to take it back out again." Holding Ron's gaze steadily, the alpha mate ordered, "No shifting while the plate is in you, or you could really mess yourself up."

As Ron licked his lips and nodded slowly, he could practically hear his wolf whine in the back of his mind.

"How long?" Ron questioned, nearly breaking out in a cold sweat before he'd even heard the answer.

"Um." Lark hesitated. "Four to five weeks."

"Shit," Ron whispered.

He couldn't remember the last time he'd gone that long without connecting with his wolf.

Easing closer, Miles wrapped his arms around his torso.

"I'll help you get through this, my mate."

Ron rested his head against his mate's chest, allowing his heady scent to soothe him. Feeling another hand sliding into his right hand, he spotted Markus offering him a sympathetic smile and nod.

I have people who have my back to help me.

CHAPTER NINE

"Stop it," Miles growled, frowning at Ron. "Just wait for me to come around and get that."

Ron huffed, the peppery smell of his frustration teasing Miles's nostrils. "I have crutches, you know."

Over the last week and a half, while Miles and Ron had been staying at Alpha Declan's, Miles had focused on learning the meaning of different scents. Fortunately, the alpha had been very accommodating in helping him. After all, all Declan had needed to do was point out the different notes that polluted Ron's scent whenever he felt certain things.

To Miles's relief, after the second or third time, Ron had finally caught on that Alpha Declan was trying to train Miles. That allowed Ron to feel whatever the hell he wanted, from angry to frustrated to annoyed, and he never needed to try to temper himself. Ron could let out all his varying degrees of frustrations, pains, and even happiness, and that had ended up being educational for Miles.

Miles had been relieved to give Ron something that made him feel useful while he was laid up in bed . . . even as odd as it seemed.

After nearly two weeks, they were finally returning to Ron's house.

Our house, I guess.

Miles could only hope that, given enough time, it would feel like home. As he'd only been there a couple of times over the last nearly two weeks, the place still felt strange to him. At one point, Miles had left Ron in Markus's care, so he could meet with Anthony at the house.

Ron's boss had delivered some of the groceries that Miles had left in the back of the truck. The frog shifter had kept the perishables—the vegetables and other items that needed refrigeration. Anthony had delivered the canned and frozen items . . . minus the ice cream. Evidently, seeing that it had been kept in the department refrigerator for several days, the ice cream had been eaten by Nathan, Markus, Warren, and a new hire—Goliath Dickman.

While Miles and Ron had both gotten a kick out of his name, Anthony had warned them never to comment on it. Evidently, Nathan had done just that, and Goliath had had him by his throat in seconds. Only Warren and Anthony's paranormal strength—even when they were pretending to be weak—had loosened the massive human's hold and pulled him back.

Goliath was right because the human was huge—six-foot-eight. As long as he wasn't teased about his name, Anthony assured that he was very easy-going. Hell, there was even a note in his file about never commenting on it.

From what Anthony had shared, the reason Goliath had chosen to move had been to get a fresh start. He'd been stuck with the shittiest shifts and patrol areas because the wrong detective had taken offense when Goliath had told him to piss off when he had—not so nicely—asked if he had a goliath dick.

Assholes are alive and well everywhere.

"Oh," Sheriff Anthony had added as if an afterthought. "And he's asking to be called Ollie . . . so don't forget."

While Miles had saluted, Ron had grinned and nodded.

Now, finally, Miles was moving Ron back into his own home. "Just stay there, damn it," Miles grumbled as he rushed from the SUV and hurried around it. "Yes, you have crutches now, but this is gravel, and that's new to you."

In order to finally leave Alpha Declan's lodge, they'd

needed to wait until Ron had gotten the cast off his left wrist. That had happened the day before. Lark had insisted on a day for Ron to practice with the crutches before leaving.

Miles knew that Ron was over the moon to be home, but he didn't need his mostly healed mate to face-plant it in the gravel first thing.

How am I going to fuck him through the mattress if we have to head back to Alpha Declan's?

Besides, not taking care of his mate would feel like a failure to both him and his cat.

As it was, Miles's cat wasn't exceptionally happy with him. Due to the fact that Ron couldn't shift, he was keeping his own beast under wraps. Miles didn't feel right flaunting his animal when Ron couldn't let his own out.

As much as Miles's cat understood, he was bored as hell. For the most part, all they did was sit around and take care of Ron. Part of that was fulfilling. Unfortunately, it also led to many long, slow days.

Miles had taken the time to help Warren and Nereo move out of Declan's. Markus had stayed with Ron then, too. To Miles's pleasure, his buddy had found a home only half a mile from Ron's.

They'd also snuck in a run while in cheetah form — Nereo using vampire speed to keep up with them — for a short while anyway.

Reaching the SUV's passenger side, Miles frowned when he found Ron already standing beside the vehicle. He had his crutches under his arms, and he looked ready to start heading to the house. That meant getting up three steps to a porch that didn't have a railing.

Ron shot a frown Miles's way, as if he knew what he was thinking. "I waited for you," he muttered. "Now you can trail after me like the good kitty cat you are, ready to catch me if I fall."

"If you weren't on crutches, I'd smack your ass," Miles shot back. Then he watched how Ron moved, catching his mate's scathing look over his shoulder at him. After shutting the passenger door, Miles stalked after Ron. His shifter was becoming just a little too irritable. "In fact." As soon as Ron planted his crutch forward and began shifting his weight, Miles smacked his ass hard enough to cause a good sting. Hearing his mate's growl and seeing his snarl, Miles pointed a finger at him and called him out. "You deserved that. You're being a dick."

Freezing, Ron stared at him with wide eyes for a few seconds. Then he hung his head, sagging on his crutches. "Sorry," he mumbled.

Hating how dejected Ron appeared, Miles slid his arm around his waist. "Let's get inside," he urged before bussing a kiss to his neck. "Then you can tell me what has such a bee in your boxers."

Ron lifted his head and arched a brow at him. "Don't you mean bonnet?"

Miles snorted. "Do you wear a bonnet?" he asked pointedly.

Waggling his brows, Ron purred huskily, "I can assure you, I don't wear boxers, either." He winked, then began crutching forward carefully as he tossed over his shoulder, "Or any other kind of underwear."

Groaning, Miles lowered a palm to his groin. His cock began to quickly fill behind his fly. He'd worked so hard to be good while at the alpha's . . . more because Ron was injured than because he was worried about what the alpha would think if he fucked his mate through the mattress every night and twice on Sundays. After all, Warren and Nereo had bonded in the alpha's house, and they'd been living there for months afterward while Nereo had helped the others.

Declan didn't care if others fucked in his home . . . as long as it was in privacy.

"I can't wait to explore that statement," Miles rumbled as he followed Ron at a large enough distance as to not get in the way of his mate's movements. A thought struck him. "Is that why you're so cranky? You horny?"

Growling under his breath, Ron snapped a glare in his direction. "As if you don't know." He eased up the first step, then the second. While rising to the deck proper, he grumbled, "You've been rebuffing my every advance." Then Ron glared at him again. "You won't even sleep in the same bed as me."

Groaning at his own ineptitude, Miles hurried past Ron to open the front door. "Get in here," he urged gruffly. "I'm sorry I made you feel that way." As Miles watched Ron crutch into his home's comfortable front room, he hurried to admit, "I've never been in a relationship, and I don't know shit about how to read signals." Miles shut the door and locked it before turning and resting his back against it so he could keep an eye on Ron. "I'm sorry my ineptitude made you think I don't want you. Especially when just the opposite is true."

"The opposite?" Ron carefully turned on his crutches to face him. Questions lit up his hazel eyes, making the green speckles within seem to dance with some inner light. "Then you do want me?"

"We're fucking mates. I claimed you," Miles snarled, stalking forward as frustration filled him. "How the hell can you think I don't want you?" Resting his hands on Ron's shoulders, Miles dipped his head so he could look into his wolf shifter's eyes . . . and he hated the uncertainty he saw within their depths. "Yes, I want you." Going with his usual blunt nature, Miles stated, "I want to carry you to the bedroom, lay you down on the bed, and fuck you until we both pass out from pleasure." Miles could feel his cat rumbling with excitement as his arousal began to stir, heating him from the inside out. "We'll lie sweaty, messy, and spent within each other's arms, running the risk of passing out so we wake sticking to each other."

Ron groaned loudly, the heady scent of his arousal rolling off of him in thick waves. "Yessss," his wolf hissed, holding his gaze. "Yes, now."

Miles groaned and nodded. Unable to deny that request, he lunged forward and swept Ron into his arms. Cradling his wolf shifter close to his chest, Miles paid no attention when the crutches clattered to the hardwood floor.

Ever-so-carefully, Miles turned in the hallway so he didn't accidentally thump Ron's leg cast against anything. He reached the master bedroom, pausing only long enough for Ron to open the door. Then Miles rushed inside and laid his mate on the bed.

After a couple of sweeps of his gaze down and over Ron's body, Miles went to work on his mate's clothes. He wore only a light jacket and a shirt on his top. The bottom required a bit more finesse, since he had to maneuver sweat pants down his legs and over his right cast. Miles didn't know when Ron had done it, but somewhere along the way, he'd ditched the shoe on his left foot. He took the man's sock off with the sweats.

Other than his cast, Ron lay bare before Miles. Finally, he felt a fissure of nerves pierce the lust that had been driving him. Talking about something in theory and discussing tips with his buddies was completely different than actually doing it.

I can do this. I want to do this.

Ron eased to a sitting position and gripped his hand in a loose hold. "You okay?"

Refocusing on Ron, Miles scoffed softly as he smiled at him. "I've thought about this, imagined how it would go, even dreamed about it." After swallowing hard, Miles admitted, "Now that I'm here, I'm feeling those nerves in my belly that have me worrying about my ability to please you."

Squeezing Miles's hand, Ron told him, "As long as I'm in your arms, you'll be pleasing me."

"God." Miles drew his hand away from Ron. Even as he acknowledged the confused narrowing of his mate's eyes, he quickly began stripping his own clothes. Once he stood naked as the day he was born, Miles met Ron's gaze and smiled hungrily at him. "You do know how to stroke a man's ego."

"Only yours."

Miles growled, liking that response more than he could say. He turned to the nightstand and opened the middle drawer. When he'd met Anthony there to put away the groceries, he'd taken a few extra minutes to snoop around the place. Miles knew where Ron kept his lube.

He'd also discovered a few toys, but he hadn't said a word about them to his buddies. Instead, he wanted to wait until Ron was well enough to share them with him. After several long weeks together—*nothing like having to do nothing but talk while letting a guy heal to get to know someone*—Miles knew he would be able to trust his mate . . . with all things.

Straightening, Miles drew the lube from the drawer, then closed it. He climbed onto the bed and slowly stretched out beside Ron. "So," he began slowly, nerves riding him hard. "I know I can't pound you into the mattress." He met Ron's wince with a rueful expression of his own. "No matter how much we both want it. We'll do it first thing after your cast is off." With a wink, Miles tried to hide his uncertainty by asking for direction from Ron. "So, you're in a cast from mid-thigh down. What's the easiest way to do this?"

"I've been giving that a lot of thought," Ron revealed. Then he glanced around before grabbing a couple of pillows. "I'll need to keep my casted leg out of the way and without pressure, so uh . . ." Ron focused on Miles and admitted, "I can't take your weight. No matter how much I want to feel you pressing me into the mattress." His cheeks took on a pink hue as he admitted, "I just can't right now."

"It's fine, my mate," Miles assured. His nerves began to ease as he realized that he wasn't the only one uncertain. Taking Ron's hand, he lifted it to his lips and pressed a light kiss to his palm. Miles racked his brain for a good position, which was made difficult by the throbbing in his hard cock. "How about I prop your hips on a pillow and your leg on a couple more? Will that work?" Then he quickly added, "Unless you don't like face-to-face?"

Miles remembered Warren and Bailey discussing how every man had preferences and things they didn't like about fucking.

Personally, Miles would love the opportunity to kiss while screwing. He'd always enjoyed kissing. Considering the way Ron had pounced on him and made out with him several times, he hoped he was right in assuming that his wolf wouldn't mind face-to-face sex.

Ron moaned softly even as he nodded eagerly. "That would be perfect," he told him huskily. "Damn perfect." With a groan, he used his left leg to push off the bed so he could shove a pillow under his ass. "Any fucking way would be perfect."

With a growl, Miles pounced on Ron, stopping him from doing any more of the work. He carefully arranged his mate's legs, spreading them, and getting him comfortable. Miles found he relished the simple act of caring for Ron, and it even ramped up his anticipation and arousal.

Miles grinned as he stared at Ron, his heart thudding wildly in his chest upon seeing his wolf shifter spread and waiting, hunger in his expression.

When Ron growled and lifted his arms, reaching for him while snapping, "Hurry the fuck up," Miles quickly popped the cap on the lube. He poured a large dollop onto his fingers before closing it again.

After Miles spread it over his fingers a little, warming it as he'd been instructed by his friends, he lowered the hand to Ron's puckered opening. He hesitated an instant. Then Miles pushed through his trepidation, touched the tip of his middle finger to Ron's opening, and pushed in . . . and in.

Heat and pressure wrapped around Miles's digit, and he moaned, imagining what that exquisite pressure would feel like around his dick.

Soon!

CHAPTER TEN

Groaning softly, Ron barely resisted trying to rock into Miles's gentle — if a bit tentative — ministrations. Every tease over his sensitive inner walls felt beyond amazing. The muscles in his stomach jumped, and trembles worked through him with each brush over his prostate.

The teasing glances weren't consistent, telling of Miles's inexperience. For some reason, that made each slight glide feel even better. Ron knew that this was the first time that his mate had ever done this . . . and he was doing it to him.

"A second finger," Ron urged when he could barely keep from writhing. "I'm ready."

Miles nodded once and obeyed. His brows were furrowed deeply as he pressed a second finger in beside the first. He seemed to be analyzing every response Ron gave to his touches.

With that thought in mind, Ron opened his mouth and stopped fighting his need to moan, writhe, and beg for more.

Immediately, Miles seemed to gain confidence. He fucked Ron with his fingers faster and harder. His crooked fingertips nailed Ron's prostate more often. Even the way he massaged and glided his other hand over every inch of Ron's body became bolder. Miles even gripped Ron's cock and jerked it in slow pulls in time with his two fingers in his ass.

Wait. No. Three now.

Ron didn't know when Miles had added a third finger, but he loved the feel of the stretch. "More," he urged. "I need more." Gripping Miles's shoulders, Ron caught his cheetah's

81

gaze. "I need you *now*."

Miles froze for several seconds before he jerked a nod. With more care than Ron thought possible at that point, his mate eased his fingers free of his chute. He even took a couple of seconds to grab the lube and pour some directly onto his dick. When Miles hissed at the obvious chill, Ron nearly chuckled, but then his cat shifter met his gaze and pinned him with a feral gaze.

Oh, yeah. This's what I want.

As much as Ron wished he could spread his legs wider, he couldn't. The pillows Miles had positioned around his right leg kept him held in place. Still, he lifted his arms and beckoned with his fingers.

"Come to me, Miles," Ron urged huskily. "I want to feel you sliding in and out of my body, burrowing deeply, stretching me wide."

Ron's words seemed to do the trick.

Miles groaned roughly, the sound coming from deep in his throat. Levering over him quickly, he got into position. Ron rested his hands on Miles's shoulders, rubbing the hard, smooth flesh, as he watched his mate grip the base of his dick and position his head at Ron's hole. Then Miles lifted his head and met Ron's gaze, his expression questioning.

"Now," Ron urged, answering his silent query. "Take me now. Make me yours." He could feel his wolf beneath the surface, and his voice filled with a rough growl. "Claim me. Bond us for eternity."

"Will you bite me? Claim me, too?"

Surprised by Miles's unexpected question, Ron hesitated. Was his mate worried about that?

Miles's brows furrowed, and he muttered, "I want you to, but if you're not ready, I'll try to—"

"Stop." Ron slapped his palm over Miles's lips. "Stop." He softened his order while smiling widely at his mate. "I want to claim you, too, with everything in me and my wolf. I'm so glad you want that, too."

A wide smile curved Miles's lips. "Good."

With that one word, Miles seemed to be done with waiting. He repositioned his cock head and thrust.

Ron moaned, remembering to push out, reveling in the exquisite stretch as Miles pressed in . . . and in . . . and in. His mate was bigger than he'd anticipated. Relishing the stretch and burn, Ron did his best not to squirm, but he'd never felt so open before.

Knowing that this was Miles's first time coupling with a man, knowing that he would be the only man to ever feel the burn of his delicious cock, Ron felt his own body hurtling toward the edge. He groaned, which caused Miles to pause and stare down at him in question.

Sliding his hands up Miles's wide shoulders, Ron smiled up at him. As he teased his fingertips along his lover's neck, in truth, he appreciated a few seconds to get used to Miles's huge shaft. His mate was definitely bigger than anything he'd ever taken, but he knew that, in a minute, he would relish every damn second of it.

"Come down and give me a kiss," Ron urged, tugging ever-so-lightly. As Miles descended toward him, Ron added, "Then thrust and fuck me while you kiss me." Growling softly, he stated, "I want to feel it all."

With a growl, Miles did exactly as Ron wanted. He sealed their lips together before thrusting his tongue into Ron's mouth. As Ron enjoyed his mate's exquisite flavor, he felt the big man begin to move within him. Miles fed Ron a grunt, then a groan, and finally a whine.

Soon enough, the more Miles moved, the more he ravished Ron's mouth while grunting, huffing, and humming his enjoyment of their coupling bodies. Ron hung on for the ride. He loved the way Miles clung to him, gripping his hair with one hand while sliding his other under his hips.

As Ron kissed Miles back, giving as good as he got, he began to lose himself in the exquisite tingles and zings created by his mate's dick sliding over his prostate over and over. His gut clenched, and his balls ached. Feeling his orgasm swell through him, Ron turned his head and broke the kiss, a groan of completion erupting from him.

Ron cried Miles's name as his body jerked with pleasure. Even the slight discomfort from the jolting shocks to his leg as Miles buried himself over and over into his ass couldn't stop him from swimming pleasantly on aftershocks and endorphins. When Ron felt his gums ache, he didn't fight it. He opened his mouth, allowing his canines to extend.

Then Ron sank his teeth deep into the flesh where Miles's neck met his shoulder. His mate's blood welled up around his teeth and flowed across his tongue. As soon as Ron tasted his forever love's exquisite flavor, he groaned and sucked for more, swallowing as quickly as it filled his mouth, unable to get enough of his mate's delicious nectar.

As Ron claimed his mate, he recognized the feel of Miles shaking in his grip, telling him that Miles came . . . probably more than once.

Finally, Ron gathered enough brain cells to ease his teeth free of Miles's flesh. He moaned as he swallowed once more before licking over his mate's neck again, sealing his wounds. Easing back, Ron spotted the deep claiming scar he'd left behind and grinned happily.

"Feeling smug, are you?" Miles's voice sounded thick with lethargy.

"Yeah," Ron replied, unable to deny his feelings.

Miles chuckled roughly for a few seconds. "You should." Then he slowly eased backward, pulling free of Ron's body. Before easing to his left side, Miles pushed the pillows aside, helping him get more comfortable. "I should get a washcloth," Miles muttered even as he wrapped his arms around

Ron's body and cuddled him close.

Ron chuckled softly, pressing a kiss to his mate's lips. "Well, you did say you wanted to wake up sticking together," he whispered into Miles's ear.

When all Ron got in return was a soft snore, he chuckled. As he grabbed a throw blanket and spread it over them, he realized he'd made his mate pass out from a claiming bite, too.

Mmmm . . . exchanging mating bites will be oh-so-much fun.

Sitting at the dining room table the next day, freshly fucked and then showered, Ron appreciated the cushion under his ass. He relaxed with his cup of coffee as he watched Miles prepare breakfast. Ron would never admit it to his mate, but his cheetah's culinary skills weren't all that good.

Ron hoped to be able to take over the kitchen soon.

"Hey, do you like to grill?" Ron asked suddenly.

"I do," Miles confirmed. The toaster popped, and he turned his attention to buttering the toast. "How much butter do you like?"

Seeing as they'd spent the last nearly two weeks at Alpha Declan's, they hadn't needed to do much in the way of cooking. While Miles had noted how Ron took his coffee, he hadn't caught on to other things. It wasn't as if Ron could butter his own toast.

No wonder he asked. What if I actually preferred my toast dry, and I was just being polite?

"Extra butter," Ron requested, flashing a wide smile his mate's way. He knew the ex-soldier was trying.

Gods, he's taking such fantastic care of me. I really need to remember that before I start snipping.

Ron had always been a shit patient. He didn't get sick, but the few times he'd had an injury . . . yep, he knew he'd been a jerk about it. Loving being active and the outdoors so much, Ron had a hard time sitting still.

Healing sucked.

"I know you're bored as hell," Miles stated, setting a plate of food before him. There was bacon, over-easy eggs, and a hashbrown patty. It looked and smelled delicious. "How about a walk this afternoon?"

Unable to help himself, Ron dug into the food. He'd taken nearly half a dozen bites before he registered Miles's question. "Wait, you—" He paused, stopping his attempt to speak around a mouthful of food. Once he'd swallowed and his mouth was empty, Ron asked, "You want to go for a walk?"

Miles smiled warmly at him. "Yeah. I bet a stroll would help ease how cooped up your wolf must be feeling right about now." After shrugging one big shoulder, he muttered, "Sitting on a back deck can only do so much good."

Ron groaned as he nodded. "So true." Grinning at Miles, he stated enthusiastically. "I would totally love a walk. I seriously need some nature."

Smiling widely, Miles pointed at the food. "Then eat up. I don't want to worry about you going hungry."

With something to look forward to, Ron began chowing with gusto. It helped that it seemed that breakfast was something Miles didn't have a problem cooking. The hashbrown patty was crunchy on the outside and soft on the inside. The bacon had just the right amount of crispy. Even the toast had the perfect amount of butter.

Ron even asked for seconds, anticipating how strenuous a walk on crutches would be.

As Ron relaxed at the table, nursing a third cup of coffee, he enjoyed watching his sexy Miles move around the kitchen.

Yeah, this is a morning routine I could get used to.

And it'll get even better when he'll let me join him in washing the dishes.

After the kitchen had been cleaned, Miles helped Ron onto a chaise lounge on the back deck. He had to take a few

86

minutes to brush the cushions free of leaves before helping Ron lever onto it. Then Miles pressed a kiss to his lover's lips.

"Give me a few minutes to change, and I'll be right back out," Miles rumbled, holding out Ron's coffee to him. He'd carried the cup so Ron hadn't spilled. "Then we'll take a stroll. A little physical activity will do you good."

Ron couldn't agree more. "I look forward to it."

Even if it gives me a few bruises under my armpits from the damn crutches.

As long as Ron got a little *alone* time with his mate, he didn't care what it cost. He'd lived by himself for decades. Living in someone else's house, even under doctor's orders, had begun to chafe like nothing he'd ever imagined.

Coupled with not being able to turn into his wolf, Ron needed a little alone and nature time — *other than my mate, of course. He's always welcome.*

Relaxing on the deck, Ron took slow, deep inhales of air. He relished the wonderful clean mountain freshness. There was nowhere else he'd been able to find it.

Wait a minute. What is that floral scent?

Floral?

The day of being caught in a pig snare came at him fast. Where he knew that scent from finally slammed into him.

Oh shit.

"Ah, ah, ah, Ron." Michelle sauntered around the corner. She held what looked like a tranquilizer gun in her hand. Pointing it at him, she held it steady on Ron as she slowly climbed the back deck's steps. "I wondered when your new protector would let you out of his sight." Michelle shook her head as she curled her lip at him. "I knew it was just a matter of time before you fags grew cocky."

Aaaand, that's where I knew the floral smell from. Michelle always enjoyed wearing different perfumes with flowery base scents.

The fact that Michelle didn't use a single particular one explained why Ron hadn't been able to connect the dots. He mentally kicked himself. If he'd just put the pieces together when he'd spotted Michelle in the office weeks before.

Except . . .

"What the hell are you doing, Michelle?" Ron asked slowly, still scrambling mentally. "You're not the one who drove me off the road."

Smirking, Michelle rolled one slender shoulder. "I have plenty of cousins," she said by way of explanation.

"Michelle," a masculine voice barked. "Hurry up and ask him where Baxter is." A big guy came creeping around the side of the house and into view. "We gotta shoot him and get outta here."

"Relax, Moris," Michelle responded with a wave of her hand. "We'll find your brother."

That explains so much. The pair has to be brothers.

Wondering what was keeping his mate, Ron tried to buy some time. "What'd Michelle promise you, Moris?" he asked, turning his focus on the guy. "What'd she promise you and Baxter?" Ron tried to sound reassuring as he forced a smile while looking at Moris. "We just want to live our lives. Ya know? Surely you can understand that."

Ron wasn't so certain Moris could actually understand anything. The hulking dude had a squashed face and mean, squinty eyes. He also had a crooked nose that looked like he'd been in his share of fights. The guy didn't scream *understanding*.

Moris curled his lip as he scowled at Ron. "You gonna give me a hundred thousand dollars?" Without waiting for a response, he smiled creepily as he focused on Michelle. "Now can I beat him? I told you shifters heal a hell of a lot faster, and now you can see what I meant after all the injuries he got when I ran him off the road." His laughter sounded cold and mean as he cracked his knuckles. "I'd love to see what else he could take."

Well shit.

CHAPTER ELEVEN

As Miles pulled on a fresh pair of jeans, the hairs on the back of his neck stood on end. Slowly buttoning and zipping, he cast a surreptitious glance toward the windows. He didn't see anything outright.

Except, between Miles's military training, which screamed that there was trouble, along with his new senses as a shifter that told him to get back to his mate, he knew something wasn't quite right. He grabbed a clean polo shirt from the dresser drawer before heading into the bathroom. In there, he stepped into the tub he hadn't yet had the opportunity to use. Miles carefully cracked the window.

With his back against the wall, Miles waited and listened, straining his ears.

For a long moment, Miles heard nothing. He began to second-guess himself. He'd just reached out to close the window when he heard a masculine voice grumble something under his breath.

Miles carefully peered out the window and just caught the flash of dark clothing disappearing around the side of the house. Quickly climbing out of the tub, he hurried through the house. He had to check each window to make certain that whoever was out there didn't see him.

By the time Miles reached the rear of the home and had a view of the back deck, an older woman stood there. She was holding a tranquilizer gun on Ron, and there was an ugly smile curving her lips. Miles felt his fingers twitch, and he decided he really needed Castrose to teach him how to read lips.

I'd much rather never see Ron in danger again, but seeing as he's a deputy, I guess I won't get that wish for a while.

Wait. A deputy . . .

Miles pulled his phone from his pocket and called Crew. "What's wrong?"

Miles appreciated Crew's assumption. "Two known in-truders here—one male. One female. You with Anthony?"

"Yeah."

"Female's picture coming through." Miles took a picture of the woman on the deck and sent it before returning the phone to his ear. "Does your man know where Ron keeps his service weapon?"

Miles really needed to get a couple of guns of his own. Having served for so long in the military, he knew his way around weaponry. Miles missed having a pistol of his own.

After I get Ron out of this, I'm going to talk to Prier about getting me something.

"This is Anthony." Crew's mate's tenor voice came through the line. "That's Michelle Laraby. You said there was a man?"

"Just caught a glimpse of him," Miles replied softly, watching Michelle speaking to Ron. He recognized the name. "Big, hulking guy." That description jogged Miles's memory, and he quickly added, "Most likely the driver of the truck." Putting pieces of the puzzle together quickly, Miles guessed, "Perhaps the ex-sheriff left his truck with Michelle rather than driving it all the way to Wyoming."

"Maybe. Crew is using my phone to call in the cavalry," Anthony told him. "Keep your man safe."

"Where does Ron keep his service weapon?" Miles asked again.

Miles tensed as he waited for an answer, seeing the bruiser come into view. The guy was leering at Ron, but not in an, *I want to fuck you*, way. No, the guy was cracking his knuckles as if imagining how much damage he could do to Ron.

So not happening. I'll rip out his throat first.

"I have his service weapon here," Anthony revealed, disappointing Miles. "Declan gave it to me while Lark was operating on Ron's leg. We're ten minutes out. Some of the others might be closer."

Seeing the big man begin stalking closer, Miles muttered, "Gotta go. Line open." Then he placed the phone on the table.

Miles thought quickly, trying to decide the best way to save his mate. Hearing his cat snarl in his mind, he quickly stripped. He crouched and urged his cheetah to come forward, allowing the shift to take over.

Once Miles stood on four paws, he peeked around the corner again just in time to see Michelle raise her weapon and aim at Ron.

"Where's Baxter?" the big man was screaming, his deep voice easily heard even through the closed glass door. "Where's my brother?"

Miles didn't think Ron could answer that question. While waiting for his mate to wake after surgery, Declan had stopped by and talked to him about the guy. After doing another sweep of Baxter's mind, Nereo had wiped all his memories that pertained to shifters and Ron. Then the vampire had shut down the human's mind, essentially putting him in a coma. Nereo and Warren had taken Baxter to a hospital in Colin City, having him admitted as a John Doe. In a month or so, Baxter would wake with no memory of how he'd gotten there or why. As Miles hadn't discussed that with Ron, yet, he knew his wolf wouldn't be able to tell the angry brother anything.

That's okay. These guys don't need to know until Nereo has a chance to strip their minds. Then Miles saw Michelle's features draw down in a sneer, and she lifted the tranquilizer gun. *If I leave them alive.*

With that thought in mind, Miles galloped around the corner. He picked up speed. At the last second, he ducked his head and hunched his shoulders. Slamming into the sliding glass door, Miles went right through it, ignoring the possibility of cuts from flying glass.

Miles heard Michelle scream. From the corner of his eye, he spotted her acting on instinct. She lifted her arms to cover her face.

Perfect.

That meant she was no longer aiming the gun at Ron. Barreling into Michelle, he barely resisted the urge to pounce on her and rip out her throat. Only Miles's uncertainty as to who was the mastermind behind everything stayed his claws and teeth.

Still, Miles's hit sent Michelle falling and tumbling. She ended up on the ground, crumpled in a heap. The smear of blood on her temple as well as her still form told him that at some point during her fall, she'd hit her head on something hard enough to knock her out.

A sharp sting hit Miles's flank.

Miles glanced at his side and spotted the red feathering of a tranquilizer dart.

Well shit.

While waiting for the expected wave of dizziness to swamp him, Miles bared his teeth at the guy.

"Miles," Ron cried, leaning forward in his deck chair. Worry filled his hazel eyes.

"Is that this abomination's name?" the guy asked. "Can't wait to enjoy two play things." Then the man turned the weapon on Ron.

"Wait a minute, Moris," Ron murmured, lifting his hands in placation. "If you give me a phone, I can call and get Baxter's location. Isn't that what you want?"

"I'll find him without you," Moris claimed, scowling. "No way I'm letting you give away the fact that we're here."

To Miles's surprise, he felt nothing—no sleepiness, sluggishness, or fatigue. *Go figure.* Crouching, he lunged at the man.

Moris ended up being surprisingly agile. He pivoted while taking a step back, and Miles missed him. As Miles landed and immediately turned to launch at him again, he felt another prick of a tranq dart.

At the same time, Miles saw Ron swing his crutch like a club. It hit the big man just above his knees. Moris grunted and turned back to Ron. With a roar, the large man backhanded Ron, sending his unbalanced mate sprawling from his chair.

Hearing Ron's cry of pain, clearly jostling his casted leg, Miles roared and launched at Moris again. Moris lunged off the deck into a dive forward roll, and once again, Miles missed him. Sliding on the deck planks, Miles dug in his claws to stop himself.

Miles turned toward Moris again, only to find himself facing the barrel of a real gun.

"You shifters think you're so powerful," Moris snarled, hate blazing from his dark eyes. "But I've been hunting your kind for years." His smile turned creepy as he continued, "Imagine my surprise when Michelle contacted me about the abominations that got her fired." Moris chuckled coldly. "And she meant fags, but one day in the area, and I knew what you really were. Time to say good-bye."

The report of a gun caused Miles to tense as he waited for the pain of a bullet hitting him. It wouldn't be the first time. He'd been nailed more than once in the line of duty, but it never got easier.

Except, Moris ended up screaming. The gun flew from his hand as blood sprayed across the deck. The thick iron scent perfumed the air as Moris jerked his hand to his chest as he glanced around wildly.

Miles had just enough time to register that someone had shot off a couple of the man's fingers before Moris took off to the left. Torn between pursuing and staying with his mate, Miles hesitated.

Another cheetah skidded into view directly in front of Moris, snarling viciously, and Miles recognized David in animal form. The big human stumbled to a stop before starting to back up slowly. He once again looked around, obviously searching for an escape.

"Don't do it," a deep voice called just before an older, bearded man in faded jeans and a flannel jacket eased between trees and into view. He held a revolver in a sure grip, and he stared coldly at Moris. "Get down on your knees, or the next thing you'll lose will be a couple of your toes."

Moris obeyed, albeit slowly.

"Hi, Miles," the guy greeted. "Heard you needed some help, and we were in the area." As he spoke, the man never took his attention off of Moris. "How's Ron?"

After another glance at David, who was shifting, Miles realized the guy had to be Corporal Brian Haas, his friend's reclusive partner. The human had also been a medic on Ronan's team before embracing the life of a prepper. That had been before Ronan had asked Brian for help with Bailey, culminating in him dragging his fellow marine into the paranormal world.

Over the course of the couple of weeks he'd been at Alpha Declan's with Ron, all his buddies had dropped by to visit them. So had their mates. The only one who hadn't was Brian. The man didn't leave his homestead all that often, from what David had told him.

But I'm grateful that he did for this.

Initiating his own shift, Miles returned to human form. Careful of the glass from the door, he crossed to Ron's side. He knelt beside his quiet mate and gently turned him.

"Hey, babe," Miles murmured, threading his fingers through Ron's thick dark hair. "How are you doing?"

"Why does hitting a broken leg feel so much worse than

when you actually do it?" Ron growled through gritted teeth. He glanced up at him and winced. "Damn asshole."

Sliding his arms under Ron, Miles carefully lifted him. "Want me to get you a pain pill?" he offered. Lark had explained that the meds he'd given Ron were specially designed for paranormals, made by himself and another scientist.

Ron nodded as Miles settled him back on his deck chair. "Just half." Then he glanced around and added, "And some sweats for you and David."

Miles chuckled softly as he nodded. "Be right back." After pecking his lips once more, he straightened and turned toward David and his mate. "Brian?"

"Yep," the bearded human replied, confirming his identity.

"You okay here with Moris for a minute?"

Brian smirked. "Yep."

After dipping his chin in a nod of thanks to David and Brian, Miles hurried inside. He grabbed two pairs of sweats and quickly yanked one set on. With the second pair over his shoulder, he slid his feet into a pair of moccasins. Then Miles grabbed the half a pain pill for Ron as well as a bottle of water.

When Miles returned to the backyard, he saw that several others had arrived, including Alpha Declan. After giving Ron the bottled water and pain pill, he tossed the sweats to David. As his friend pulled them on, Miles took in Alpha Declan forcing a bound—and bandaged, as someone had given the asshole first aid, probably Brian—to his feet.

As Enforcer Kade led Moris away, the guy frowned at Miles and yelled, "What are you?"

Miles scowled at the guy. "What are you talking about?"

Moris jutted his chin toward the discarded tranquilizer gun. "I shot you twice, and it didn't even slow you down."

Smirking, Miles replied, "I'm a science experiment."

After all the shit the scientists had pumped into his system, Miles figured a standard tranquilizer dart, even one geared toward a shifter, must not have even registered to his fucked-up systems.

While Moris frowned in obvious confusion, Kade continued leading him away. Enforcer Manon scooped up Michelle and followed the other pair.

"He admitted to being a hunter," Miles told Alpha Declan as he urged Ron to sit forward a little. He couldn't resist holding his mate for a second longer. After settling behind Ron in the chair, bracketing him with his thighs and holding him tight to his chest, Miles returned his focus to the alpha. "He claimed to have killed many of our kind."

Huh. Our kind. Yup. Guess I am one of them now. A shifter.

Alpha Declan nodded once. "Then he falls under our purview. Excellent." His smile held little warmth. "I'll let ye know how things end up."

"Michelle didn't know about us until she called in her cousins," Miles added. "She thought she was asking for help with homosexuals."

Growling softly, Declan shook his head. "Bigots," he grumbled. Clearing his features, he smiled as he turned his attention to David and Brian. "Thank ye for yer help, Brian. David." Cocking his head, the alpha asked, "How did ye end up getting here so swiftly?"

Brian grinned broadly. "We were out scouting the area when Crew's nine-one-one message came through." After sliding his weapon back into the holster on his thigh, he wrapped his arm around David's waist. "We realized how close we were and came asap."

"Again, thank ye," Alpha Declan repeated.

"We're family," David claimed softly, sliding his gaze to Miles. "It's what we do."

Miles smiled at his teammate, nodding in acknowledgment, confirmation, and acceptance.

Family.

"And family also helps clean up the aftermath," Crew

stated, rounding the side of the house with Anthony. He winced as he took in the mess on the deck. "Thought I heard you go through some glass over the phone line." Shaking his head, Crew met Miles's gaze. "You and Ron okay?"

"We're okay," Miles confirmed. Then he focused on Alpha Declan. "Can you find out if Moris told any other hunter buddies about Ron?"

Alpha Declan patted him on the shoulder. "We will, and I'll keep ye posted."

"Thank you, Alpha," Miles replied.

Ron kissed the underside of his chin, drawing Miles's attention.

Smiling at Ron, Miles asked, "You feeling better, Ron?"

Sighing and snuggling against his chest, Ron nodded. "Yeah. Now that no one is after me, I just want to cuddle with you, heal, and live happily ever after."

Miles held Ron close and whispered into Ron's ear, "Me, too, my mate. Me, too."

As Miles's buddies began cleaning up the mess from the glass, he realized his life had finally truly begun . . . and in his mind, it couldn't get much better.

ABOUT THE AUTHOR

Charlie started writing fantasy when she was eight, and after stumbling onto her first erotic romance at age nineteen, she realized her true calling. She now focuses on writing gay erotic romance, normally of the paranormal variety, with heroes of all kinds. With the help and support of her husband, Charlie finally fulfilled one of her life-long goals . . . move to acreage with her horses. You can often find her curled up with her laptop and a cup of tea or glass of wine, creating her next adventure. Charlie enjoys exploring the mountains of her new Oregon home on horseback, 4-wheeler, or motorcycle.

She can be reached at ch.richards2010@yahoo.com

Or visit her at www.charlie-richards.com.